RILLAN MACDHAI

Sympathy For the Living

This is a work of fiction set on an alternative Earth during a historical period. All characters are fictious and any resemblance to any persons living or dead or undead are either coincidental or, in the case of historical personages, the author's interpretation of how events and actions might have occurred in a fantasy timeline on a world where magick and other sentient beings might exist. Do not mistake this for the actual history of Earth.

Cover Art, Digital Manipulation, and Design Enhancements by Teanna Byerts. Original art, characters, and reproduction rights owned by Rillan macDhai and was obtained from the collection of the author.

ISBN: 9798809388351

Printed in the USA

For all my friends who've been waiting forever for 'the Book'

This one is especially for Teanna, Gillian, and Phyl – you got me started again!

And for Bill and Hilsh for additional support with proofreading, suggestions, and in slaying the carnivorous typos.

Special nods to Teel James Glenn for checking the fight scenes – before I added extra material. Any stupid actions in battle still in the story are purely the fault of the author.

Special thanks to Matthew Abrams for the use of his characters: Hrothgar and Dragonbiter.

And for my beloved Storm who made the storyboard to help me stay on track

If you are looking for "The Map," I suggest looking up a good map of Scotland, one with particular emphasis on the eastern coast from Inverness to Thurso. While you won't actually find Invercraig, you'll get an idea of the terrain, especially if you are looking with one of the online mapping programs. Yes, Scotland has lovely white sand beaches!

TABLE OF CONTENTS

GLOSSARY OF TERMS

Anglish league: 3 miles or 4.83 kilometers. Since Zero ran at his top speed until he slipped, he'd covered approximately 5 kilometers or 3.11 miles. An easy walking pace for me (the author) is about 2-2.5 miles/hour. Since Zero is about my size, let's say getting to the old military road is about 7 - 8 miles from where he left the coastal road.

Bothy: Hut or small cottage used as protection from the elements and usually open to whoever needs use it.

Company: 80 to 150 soldiers. Dyer's Company was at about 100 when it left Invar Nis to head north on the coastal road. Men started getting sick and dying shortly after leaving the city.

Favour: Token of approval or (not necessarily in this case) affection. English spelling of favor.

Gàidhlig: Actual term form Scottish Gaelic. Pronounced close to gaa-lik.

Ghouls: Most common form of embodied undead. They range in appearance from zombies to fast-moving zombies to someone you could mistake for being fully alive, except for their fondness for eating dead things. Many retain their memories and abilities from life, so spellcasters of several types can appear among them.

Hidden Roads/Hidden Ways: Paths through alternate dimensions, sometimes allowing faster or more direct lines of travel. The ones used by warmounts are often not healthy for mortals to use, but can risked if the warmount is well-disposed toward the mortals accompanying them.

Lope: Slow canter, both being a three-beat gait of a horse between a trot or pace and a gallop, usually more comfortable to ride than a trot, but not always faster.

Invar Nis: Inverness. Meaning the mouth of the River Ness.

Nyorth: Known as Njord in the Real World, Scandinavian God of wealth, fertility, the sea, and seafaring in the Vikings' religion. The father of Frey and Freya, he was likely also a Vanir, rather than an Aesir, and possibly an Aelfar or elven deity as well.

Pace: A two-beat gait where the legs on the same side move forward together. Riding a pacing horse is very comfortable and pacing is usually faster than trotting or loping. However, few horses pace naturally.

Reivers: Scottish term for (particularly cattle) rustlers/thieves.

Resurrectionist/Resurrectionists: Necroknights (particularly those from Scotland or the Elven Tirs) and some mortal Scots use this term to identify necromancers.

Rowan: Large shrub or tree with very tart yet edible red/orange berries that can be made into jams. Often planted near homes as a defense against evil magicks. Also known as Mountain Ash.

Skeletons: Mindless, fleshless (for the most part) animated bones, otherwise the same as zombies (see below). Animal and monster skeletons are possible, but rare.

Sloe: Early blooming plant related to the plum tree. Flowers appear before the leaves. Sloe berries can be made into a cordial (Sloe gin). Also known as Blackthorn.

Tack: Collective term for riding equipment used on horses and other equines, includes saddle, saddle blanket, bridle, martingales, cruppers, tie-downs, etc.

Warmount: Highly intelligent beings in the form of horses, possibly a type of undead, demon, or fay. Capable of traveling the Hidden Ways. They are often, but not always, partnered with a necroknight. Omnivorous. They have fangs as well as teeth for grinding.

Whin: Prickly (read: covered with spines/spikes) bush of the pea family found in the Isles and Europa (Great Britain in the Real World). It has vivid yellow flowers when blooming, thus yellow whin. Another name for Gorse.

Zombies: Mindless corporeal undead which can be given simple commands to follow or actively directed by necromancers and some necroknights and other greater undead. Zombies raised from animals or monsters are possible, but very rare. Some suggest necroknights' warmounts are a type of risen animal zombie; though not more than once in the presence of actual warmounts.

When an irate devil inclined to alchemy joined with a pair of demons to tweak the black boils sickness to a more virulent strain sometime in the late-1200s to mid-1300s Anno Domini, they created the Mankiller Plague. The death which followed changed our world for both woe and – no doubt, to the devil's dismay – weal.

B. Waterhouse, *Ye Effects Magickale & Arcane On ye Spreade of Pestilences & Disease*

. . . and the Caliburn Knights under the command of Sir Tercel Michael Davidson were significant in their action at the Battle of Elblings, also known as the Battle of Bloody Fires, when they managed to break the hold of the Risen Tsar on a mixed company of those Risen Knights variously referred to as Necroknights or Knights of the Red Horseman. Many of these now serve in the Armies of the Holy Hapsburg Empire or the heretical, so-called Protestant Union . . .

S. Brust, *Battles of the Germanies and the Polish-Lithuanian Kingdoms*

There have always been those uncommon undead named most often these days as necroknights. Since the re-animation of the son of Tsar Ivan, fourth of his name, of the House of Rurik, which we estimate took place some unknown time in the year of Our Lord 1587, they have become considerably more likely to be encountered, particularly in the states and kingdoms of the north-eastern section of the Continent held by the shattered divisions of Christendom. Most are still held enthrall to the self-crowned Risen Tsar, but after the battle at Elblings, the Twins and I found ourselves in technical possession of a large number of these undead warriors, freed by God's Grace and, I suspect, the battlefield death of the Necromancer Lich who had been their commander...

Physically they are much like the beings they were in life. Young Ivan has not been particular in who he takes into his ranks: men, giants, elves, dwarves, and others of the Kindred Races, indeed no differentiation exists among them, of race nor of gender. Likewise, any can rise (and please forgive the pun) among their ranks to become Warleaders – their term for generals.

While many of them are difficult to immediately identify as something other than the commonly animate corpses we refer to as ghouls, I have noticed after several years of studying the more powerful among them becoming more and more the image of who they were in life. This is not a universal truth, some seem to take a perverse pleasure in retaining the most horrific of visages, while others consider it part of their penance for the vile deeds they committed in life and undeath. There are some universal similarities: vastly enhanced strength, speed, minor telekinetic ability, and regeneration of wounds through an apparently unique type of necromantic feeding upon the living or recently dead.

When injured, some are seen to bleed as do living beings, though in all cases observed, I have not seen true red blood, but rather either a thin, watery pinkish-yellow serum or a thick, dark red, almost black ooze. While this bleeding weakens them, when sorely wounded, they are known to enter berserker states where they attack until either hacked to pieces or they succeed in overwhelming their opponent and restoring themselves by necromantic and actual physical feeding as we have seen done by ghouls. The most certain ways to return them to death is to strike off their heads or burn them with either natural or magickal flames.

Those who now serve in the armies of the Protestant Union or of the Holy Hapsburg Empire remain united across faction divides in most case as Brethren of the Order of the Red Horseman. They frequently greet each other as Brothers or Sisters in Death. They also refer to themselves as the Free Undead. The terms are used in both the Protestant Union and the Hapsburg Empire, where they are also known as the Knights Irregular or less officially as the Knights of the Dead Horse. In the Protestant Union, they are generally referred to collectively as Knights of the Red Horseman or Knights of the Black Horseman, which leads to a certain amount of confusion, compounded by their own terms for themselves as necroknights of the Red, White, or Yellow Horses.

Necroknights of the Red Horse faction are chiefly straight up warriors or warriors-mages particularly able with fire magicks, but more likely to use common weapons in battle than to engage in duels arcane. Somewhat the opposite number to the Red Horse are the Necroknights of the White Horse. They are an odd catch-all of those who wielded the other powers arcane and those who, while having no arcane training, can imitate arcane abilities, such as the elven shadow-walkers' ability to blink across short distances as do arcane mages. They are skilled with frost and ice magicks and necromantic abilities such as creating other undead by summoning the spirits of those slain by the diseases caused by the third faction among the necroknights, the riders of the Yellow Horse. Some among the White Horse have the ability to raise those who died of more natural, normal causes as well. The final faction among the necroknights includes the aforementioned Knights of the Yellow Horse. These have truly frightening powers to spread diseases among the living, though many are also able to recognize diseases and poisons, and in some cases, reverse their effects. Like the White Horse factions, they draw members from those who had no distinctly arcane abilities while still alive. They are also the faction most likely to include former wielders of healing magicks as well.

Sir Tercel Robert Davidson, Grandmaster of the Order of Caliburn, by my hand and seal, these Ides of March

1: A DEAD MAN AND LIVING CHILDREN

Rain.

Rain alone won't kill - not usually, anyway - but rain and cold and wind will.

If you are already dead, it will still make you cold and miserable. Or colder and more miserable, as the case might be. Zerollen diGriz had been huddling under his waxed hat and riding cape for more hours than was good for him, even as a free-willed necroknight. When his warmount Bessariel planted her feet and snorted at the apparition blocking the road, he came close to pitching off over her head.

"What the hell are you thinking of, to show yourself to me?" Zero demanded of the ghostly figure standing with her arms outstretched to cover as much of the highway as possible.

The spectral woman didn't speak but turned and pointed to a farm track leading off the roadway.

Both Zero and his mount eyed the path. "What's over there that's so important?" Zero asked, but the ghost had vanished so thoroughly he could have put her presence down to seeing images made only of drizzle and mist.

But Bessariel's senses had detected the ghostly woman as well.

Frowning around at the rain, Zero twitched the reins and his black mare ambled off the highway and onto the track leading toward a fog-shrouded barn and an even more difficult to see house set back among the rocks and braes which meandered alongside the high road and the rills and burns which crossed it.

***

The farm's chickens peeped and chooked and pecked and scratched, looking for a bit of grain, grass, or a bug in the still-dry dust of the barn's doorway and under blaeberry bushes planted along its side. They darted out into the open briefly to drink from puddles, before returning to the relative warmth and dryness of the barn. A few made brave runs into the doorless shelter of the farmhouse.

Doorless, but not quite un-barricaded. What might have been a tabletop blocked the lower half of the doorway. The chickens did fluttery hops and disappeared inside.

Other than the chickens and a few smaller birds flitting among the bushes, nothing moved in the rain, though occasionally he had heard a cow bawling her complaints to the dreary morning.

His mount - free-willed herself, and tired of the downpour - shoved him with her nose and walked past, heading determinedly toward the barn.

"All right, Bessariel," he agreed. "Might as well stir the hornet's nest and see what flies out."

The black mare flicked an ear back at him and continued into the barn, barely startling the chickens. A querulous whinny greeted her.

The still-unseen cow moaned another complaint as well.

Zero followed his mare to the barn, keeping a wary eye on the house. A mostly white rooster had hopped up on the tabletop barricade and once again loudly announced it was morning and where-is-the-food to the steading and all surrounding areas.

Inside the barn, Bessariel was doing sniffy-squealies over a stall door with what was either a skinny old plow horse or a very starved warmount. The chickens scattered, then closed in around his feet as Zero approached the pair. A particularly bold or hungry chicken went so far as to peck at his riding boots. The now-visible wooly cow shook her ball-tipped horns at him and bawled her complaints loudly enough in the confines of the building to make him wince.

"Okay, old woman," Zero told her. "I'll see what I can do for you. Just give me a moment to find you water and food. I'll even milk you, if you won't try kicking my head off."

"Moo-oo-oo-oo!" complained the cow, still at an ear-piercing volume.

The old horse snorted as well and rattled its trough.

"Well, thank the Gods, at least they don't seem to have any pigs," Zero told Bess. The black mare stamped a hoof and continued sniffing and nuzzling the old horse.

The cow, on closer inspection, was enormously round. Apparently, she was close to foaling or calving or whatever it was cows did when giving birth. Calving, that was the term, Zero thought. There was a big wooden bucket near her stall. Zero grabbed it and headed out to look for the farm's well.

Other than the hopeful chickens following him and a few small birds hopping around in the bushes and house garden, there was still nothing moving beyond the dripping of water from sky and branch. A well-worn path, reinforced with flat stones which made irregular steps, led uphill from the barn to a walled spring. Someone had cunningly made a runoff spout with a notch just the right size to hold a bucket's bail.

Someone had also left a body face down in the catch basin, fouling the water, and blocking the runoff so the water was welling up and over the stone of the catchment.

"Are you going to get up?" Zero asked the body, suspiciously.

The body just lay there, bobbling a little in the movement of the water.

With a sigh, Zero set the bucket down and extended a hand toward the body. Purply-blue tendrils of energy reached out and probed the corpse.

Nothing happened.

Zero sighed again and relaxed fractionally. "Well, you poor bastard, let's get you out of there. Here's hoping you don't fall apart on me while I move you."

The body was not cooperative, but Zero had been on too many battlefields to be very surprised. At least it didn't *actually* fall apart. It had been human or at least more human in appearance than Zero himself. A wool jacket foul and sodden from the water and red DeNims trousers suggested the body might have been a Anglish Unionist soldier, but given the lawless state of the Empty Lands, the body could as easily have been a brigand or the farm's owner. If it was the farmer, it would certainly explain the lack of movement in the house.

"May you have passed over in peace and not too many pieces," he told the dead body while he cleaned out the spring's catch basin. After cleaning himself and judging the force of the spring had washed away the foulness remaining, he filled the bucket and took it back down to the waiting animals. The living had more need of his care than a days' dead corpse, but Zero was even colder now than he had been. He gave the house a more considering look, taking in the chimneys at either end of the building. No smoke rose from either one.

Returning to his work with the animals, he split the bucketful between the complaining cow and the old horse. A quick search out the back of the barn proved there was an attached paddock with a good amount of grass and an intact fence.

With an admonition to Bessariel to not let the old horse gorge himself sick, Zero stripped off her tack and turned all the animals out to graze. The wooly cow would just have to fend for herself, unless Bess chose to intervene. Zero wasn't certain if cows could founder like horses. At least, he didn't need to milk her immediately. From the state of her udder and what he remembered about pregnant mares 'waxing' before a birth, there would soon be a calf to take care of that problem. He'd give the animals a few minutes before he brought them more water, too.

That left him with the house to investigate. It was narrow, but there was a second story to it, which suggested the owners had been well-to-do either before or after the Risen had swept across the Highlands in search of the Dagda's Cauldron and the other treasures of the Tuatha. He frowned at the house. Despite the promise of warmth and the opportunity to get fully dry again, the lack of movement - other than the chickens and wild birds — made him feel nervous about approaching it. Something about it felt like a trap and he couldn't waste too much more time here, not with messages to deliver to the garrison at Thornhill.

He decided to refill the water bucket first. Having found the body in the spring he wasn't feeling particularly hopeful anyone was still alive in the building, but there would probably be something he'd end up needing to use water to clean. Maybe it would only be the table. Maybe he could use the water for the horses and the cow.

He knew also, once he was out of the rain and somewhere with a fire, he'd have even less desire to get soaked again.

"Okay, you," he said to the body by the spring. "I know this is a shitty thing to do to you, but I'm tired of being wet and cold. Get up and make yourself useful. I'll let you go once you've filled up the water trough."

He gestured, tendrils of purple flowing out from his hands and enveloping the body. It rose into the air, small pieces that had fallen off or been washed away returning to their places until it was - more or less - complete. The purple shifted through the spectrum to a pure gas-fire blue. There was a crack, like lightning-displaced air, and the body turned its head and glared at him from eye sockets filled with blue-purple flames.

"Fill this with water from this spring," Zero told the animated body and handed it the bucket. Impressing his will upon the newly Risen, he continued, "Take the bucket of water down this path, go into the barn, and through it to the fence gate. Pour the water into the trough beside the gate."

Continuing to visualize the entire process and share it with his servant, Zero described pouring the water into the paddock's water trough, returning to the spring to refill the bucket, and back down to the trough and continuing those actions until the trough was overflowing with water. "Then bring a bucketful to the doorway there," Zero pointed to the doorless house. "Once you have done all that, go to the side of the house, and you will be released."

The animated body nodded in understanding and began filling the bucket.

Zero tried to rub away the ache between his eyes and started down the path to the house. He hated using his power to create another undead, but sometimes expedience outweighed morals. Putting a limit on how long the spirit was bound took less energy, plus made it almost impossible for anyone to ever summon that particular soul back again. Unless it wished to return.

Having removed his last justification for avoiding the house, Zero slogged through the mud of the farmyard to the doorway and looked in. There were chickens roosting in the ground level of a small entry room. Shawls and kilts or blankets hung from hooks on the walls and a pair of buckets - smaller than the one he'd found in the barn - rested under them. The former door was lying on the floor left of center of the room, busted off its hinges, and shattered beyond easy repair. As he'd suspected, the barricade across the doorway was a small table braced across the doorway with a bench and a couple of stools holding it in place. A defender with a blunderbuss or musket or even a crossbow might have made a stand there, but Zero saw no proof anyone had.

"Hullo? Hullo the house?" Zero called, peering inside. He considered searching for other dead with his powers, but he was too tired and cold to put any effort into it. If something wanted to get up and bother him about his being there, he'd deal with it or them with his sword and axe.

Chickens squawked and flapped, hopping off the stools and bench. Several bolted madly past him to the barn. Their presence inside made it unlikely there were any mobile dead in the building.

Over their noise, he thought he heard something from further inside, a low growl underneath a dry sobbing.

Ignoring the chickens and the nagging sense a trap was about to close on him, Zero stepped over the table and started further in. In the dimly lit room beyond, he could just see living humans, children by the size of them, in makeshift beds on the floor of what was probably the kitchen. They thrashed and cried, faces and arms marred with a bright fever-rash he could see even in the dim light from a lone window.

A dark, shaggy dog appeared in the doorway to the kitchen between him and the children. The dog was definitely alive and not at all happy to see him. It raised its hackles, growling a fierce warning before he was halfway across the room.

Zero drew his sword, considering.

A dry-throated female voice croaked out, “No, Bannock. No! Be a good dog.” The dry-throated speaker immediately behind the dog continued, directing their words now to Zero. “Please don’t hurt our dog, he’s all we’ve got left.”

The dog growled again.

Another, younger, female voice called, “Water? Please, water. Is thirsty. So hot. I hurt. Da?” There was a faint thrashing sound from the kitchen. “I want Da. I’m so hot.” The younger girl began to cry weakly. “Water? Please? Water?”

“Drink?” grated a third voice. Zero thought it sounded like a boy, though it was hard to tell, between the high tones and the obvious dry raspiness of all the voices.

The dog’s growling was louder than the words of the children. “I’m going to get you water,” Zero promised and backed away until he fetched up against the table across the doorway. He managed to shove it out of the way with a foot, while he kept a wary eye on the dog.

He caught movement that was more than the rain and pivoted in time to see the animated body coming down the path with a full bucket of water. “You! Stop!”

he yelled, putting full force into the command to override the orders he'd already given.

The body turned its head to glare at him, balancing with one foot in mid-step. With care and obvious annoyance, it put its foot down and shuffled into a semblance of attention. Zero sensed there was more 'person' behind its actions and cursed softly. *Why didn't I catch he was tainted when I examined the body?*

"Bring me the water," Zero told the animated soldier. Cursing again, he added, "Do you know what happened here?"

The soldier worked what was left of his face into a grimace.

"Sick," he said in a creaky voice.

"Fell," he added after a moment. Zero snatched the bucket from his hand and steadied the man as he re-experienced his death.

"Bastard!" The undead man cursed Zero at length, intelligence and vocabulary strengthening throughout the tirade. "Why did you bring me back?"

"I needed help. I wasn't planning on keeping you," Zero told him.

"Why?" demanded the man again. He was gaining strength of personality quickly, more than Zero would have expected.

"There are living children. They need water and nursing. I can't do it all by myself."

"Fuck you. When do the Risen care about the living?" demanded the soldier. He was definitely pulling himself together.

"When we're Free Undead," Zero growled back at him. "Unless there's a resurrectionist around here, what's left of your mind should be your own." He added, mostly to himself, "Of course, I'd have the bad luck to raise someone who was already tainted."

"Well, bugger that," said the dead man, who was looking less like a water-bloated corpse by the moment. "What do you want?"

"More water, for a start. There are more buckets in the house. I'll get them for you." Zero half turned to go back inside before thinking to ask, "Was this your home?"

"No, not mine." The dead man looked toward what Zero thought was south. "My home's a long way from here. OH! And I'm hungry."

"Fuck that," agreed Zero, who'd been expecting it. He poured a rush of his own energy into the new undead with a flare of purple-blue light around them both.

"Keep filling the water trough," he ordered. "Don't kill the chickens. Or the cow. And mind the warmounts. They'll stomp you flat if you try anything with them." He ducked into the house and snatched the two buckets he'd seen there. Bannock the dog was back in the doorway to the kitchen and growled at him again.

"Stay!" he snapped at the beast. "Down! Stay!"

The dog surprised him by actually lying down. Perhaps it sensed his own hunger and cold.

He traded buckets with the undead human. "Have you remembered your name?" he asked the ghoul.

"No," replied the undead man. "I'm getting snatches of other things, but not that. You'd think you'd remember your own name."

"I'm not going to give you a name," Zero told him. "It would anchor you even more. If you remember your own, that's another thing. Let me know if you see any other living or Risen. Kindred races or not."

That exchange done, he still had to get past the dog to help the children. And maybe find out where their parents were lurking.

If he could find out where the parents were and get them taking care of the children, then maybe he could dry out, get warm, and get back on the road. There were dispatches he needed to get to the Unionist garrison at Thornhill. He hoped the ghostly woman who'd pointed him at the house wasn't the mother.

The way his luck seemed to be turning, it was all too possible.

Mulling all of this over, and with his blade still unsheathed from his first encounter with Bannock, he started to walk into the kitchen. "I've brought water," he began.

The dog launched himself at Zero, barking and snapping. The older girl ducked her head and lunged at the pair of them, her eyes squinching shut in fear. "No!"

"Ah!" said Zero as the dog slashed his upthrown shield arm, splashing water from the bucket everywhere. He staggered under the dog's weight and nearly tripped over the girl now lying at his feet. For a moment, he flailed before putting his blade into the countertop above the girl with a wicked cracking sound of old boards breaking. The sword thrummed indignantly but wedging it into the wood let him keep his feet.

The dog had let go and was working his mouth open and shut and pawing at his mouth as well, trying to get rid of the taste of necroknight flesh. Zero wiggled his sword out of the wood and lifted it out of dog and child range.

"No!" cried the boy and tried to struggle closer.

Bitten and now with two children squirming underfoot, Zero considered getting the weapon out of his hand the wisest thing he could do. Both of the older children looked surprised when the sword clattered down on what remained of the long counter under the room's single window. "Calmer now, Bannock?" Zero asked the dog, who had retreated to the other side of the girl. "I didn't taste all that good, did I?"

The shaggy dog whined uncertainly.

There was a gnawed ham on the floor and a spilled crock with the remains of butter or soft cheese near the smallest child. She was thrashing around as well, but this seemed more from the fever than concern about him.

"Is there anyone else I need to find?" Zero asked the girl at his feet. She seemed to be the senior of the three.

"Don't tell him, Aggie!" cried the boy, squirming closer. "Oh! Blessed Saint Andrew! Aggie, look at his eyes! He's one of the dead walking!"

Zero flinched, but the boy's reaction wasn't unexpected. Most living had no good way to tell the difference between the Risen and the Free Undead.

"Hush yourself, Hector," rasped Aggie. "There's nothing he can do worse than what the living already did to us."

The two younger children wailed. The older girl pushed herself up on her arms, giving Zero a challenging examination somewhere between hope and despair. Bannock bellowed a warning against coming closer, ridiculous by itself as the necroknight was practically standing on top of the girl.

"Water, please. There's no one else here," said Aggie, ignoring her brother and collapsing back down into her nest of blankets. "Our Da went to get help. But he hasn't come back. I don't know if it's only been for a day or two. We've all been so sick. Maybe longer."

"I've got water outside. I'll bring it for you."

"There's water here, in the grey crock. I just couldn't get up enough to reach it after the first day," said Aggie, shame in her voice. "I was dumb. I should have left it down. Mary-wee and Hector need it bad."

"You need it, too," said Zero.

He busied himself sharing drinks between all three of the children. All of them were feverish. He had to give them the water in sips, with time in between, as though they might colic like an overly thirsty horse. Bannock kept circling around as sheepdogs are prone to do, but a sharp "No!" from the children or even himself kept the dog from darting in and biting him again.

In between giving the children water, Zero stripped off his riding cloak and traded it for one of the tartan woven blankets hanging in the other room. The peat fire was difficult to bring back into burning, almost smothered in the ashes, but the chimney had a good draw. He managed to coax the fire to flame again without too much smoke backfeeding into the room. Soon after, warmth began spreading from the hearth.

The children were covered with red spots and splotches. While measles was nothing he had to worry about anymore, the children were already dehydrated and the worst of the fever would be hitting them soon, if it hadn't already. He'd tried moving the little girl over between her brother and older sister, but she clung to him, pressing her feverish head again his chest. He ended up carrying her around as he worked, cradled in his sore arm. Even though he wasn't carrying the weapon, experience had taught him to leave his sword hand as free as possible.

"What happened here?" Zero asked after he'd gotten the little humans water and food and begun the process of cleaning them up from lying in their own filth.

Bannock confined himself to lurking on the other side of the kitchen, alternately growling and whining at the necroknight, while Aggie explained, "Brigands. Said they were Unionist Army, but Da didn't believe them."

Hector added, "All of us took sick after they were here. Plague spreaders they were."

"Da went for the wise woman," Aggie continued. "I made us beds down here." She sobbed suddenly. "I didn't know I'd get so weak. I left the water up so Bannock wouldn't foul it with his slobber. The cheese pot had a lid, but the lid for the water crock broke a year ago, not long after Mam died."

"Shh, shh, lass," Zero soothed as best he could, flustered by her tears. He braced himself against the counter and slid down beside Aggie, cuddling her next to Mary-wee who was still clinging to him like a limpet. He hoped the dog wouldn't launch himself at him again.

"You don't understand," Aggie continued. "We were sucking water out of Bannock's fur. We'd have died if it hadn't been for him coming in wet. And pulling down the ham. And I nearly killed us by not leaving the water down. And our Da's not coming back, is he?"

"I don't know," Zerollen told her, not wanting to mention the body he'd found in the spring but seeking to comfort the girl. "How was he dressed? Maybe I've seen him."

Even though the man he'd raised thought he wasn't from this place, the newly re-animated often had spotty memories, when they had any memories at all.

"He had on his great kilt and his linen shirt," said Hector.

Zero felt some relief. Whoever had died in their spring had definitely not been dressed in tartan and linen. "You said everyone got sick. Did that include your father?"

"Da had the red rash when he was a wee un. It didn't bother him this time."

Maybe not, maybe yes, Zero thought. Though having measles once usually gave life-long protection, it didn't always. If the fever had taken their father as badly as it had the children, he might have collapsed somewhere on the road to the healer's house.

"I'm going to go get the bucket and refill your crock. Is there anything else I can put water in?"

"You can stopper the dry sink," said Aggie. "And there's bowls and more crocks in the cupboard."

Between Aggie and himself, they managed to get Mary-wee detached and nested against her sister. Aggie watched him as Zero moved around, placing the bowls carefully within reach of the children. "Are you going to leave us, too?" she asked, once he'd filled all the containers with the water bucket he'd retrieved.

Zero thought about it. He didn't have much wiggle room in his delivery schedule. But given how bad the fever was starting to hit the children, all three of them were likely to die.

They certainly would if he left. Especially if he didn't take the undead man he'd raised along with him.

And even if the children lived, the cow and horse might die or wander off before the children were well enough to care for them. Of course, the children's father might return. Or a neighbor come by to check on the farmstead.

It was too many maybes and what ifs stacked against the children's survival.

Zerollen had seen a lot of death since the Risen Tsar had led his undead horrors across the northern Highlands and Tir na Scota. Zero'd been one of those co-opted undead horrors until he'd managed to break free. Three more deaths would hardly matter in the count against him.

But elves didn't kill children, even human children. And despite his human father, he still considered himself an elf. A deenee shee. It was one of the things which had helped him break free from the Risen army.

"No," he told the children. "I'm staying."

He retrieved his sword before setting oatmeal to start soaking. By the time he was done, Bessariel was standing in the entry room, watching him and sniffing at Bannock.

The day became a round of carrying water in the rain, alongside the still-nameless ghoul. Finally buckets, basins and jars were all full, and the trough topped off again as well for the cow and horses. There was enough for cooking and drinks for the children, and to soak rags to cool their fevers. The ghoul was sent to guard the barn with a mug of hot water to sip and a dry tartan kilted around him for cover and decency while his own thoroughly sopping clothing dried. Zero sent him off with repeated orders not to eat anything or anyone.

Zero hung soiled blankets out for the rain to start cleaning. It wasn't until he'd gotten a broth of ham and oats into the children that he felt he dared strip out of his own borrowed and now soaked-through blanket and the armor he still wore underneath. He'd already rubbed down Bessariel and hung her tack to dry. He took the liberty of sharing some of the oats with her and wrapping one of the shawls which had also been hanging in the entry room around his shoulders like a cloak. He hung another blanket across the upper part of the doorway to the kitchen as he'd hung one to keep the warmth of the fire from slipping up the narrow stairwell. He leaned against the corner of the hearth, holding the shawl open to the flames until he felt in danger of igniting, then wrapped the warmed wool around himself again.

Aggie was worsening quickly. It seemed the oldest girl had held off her sickness as much as she could until his unlikely help had arrived. Now her face with bright with fever and she was beginning to thrash. With an unnecessary sigh, Zero took a soaked cloth and began wiping her face. Once he'd made a circle through the children, he re-saddled Bessariel.

"I'm sorry to send you out alone, lovely one," he told her. "But I can't bring myself to leave the smalls and this may drag on for days."

He made certain the dispatch pouch was tied and double-tied to its place behind the cantle. "Go, my Black Bess, run for Thornhill. You know the way better than I. Go to the Caliburn Great House in Thornhill."

She snorted and bunted him with her nose, refusing to leave.

He impressed his will upon her, tendrils of his power weaving around her in a gentle caress. "Go, my lovely. I'll be safe without you."

He led her to the door with a hand under her chin, pushing the blockage out of the way, and lifting back the blanket curtain he'd also placed there. "Go, Bessariel. The faster you go, the sooner you'll be back."

The mare snorted again, stamping a hoof dangerously near his foot.

"Yes," said Zero. "I'll take care of the old fellow as well. And the cow, Gods know. You've no bridle for anyone to grab, so they'll know something's happened to me. Remember to stand for them to get the messages off your saddle. And don't bite too many of them. Remember to wait to see if they'll send a search party out for me before you come running back here. If they do, go slow enough to let them keep up."

The mare gave him a side-eyed look and stepped out into the rain and shook herself. She turned her head back to her partner and stamped impatiently.

"Did you loosen the saddle?" He walked out and checked her girth. "You're fine. Go on with you," Zero told her and made a shooing motion with his hand.

She bunted him with her nose again, turned and trotted out to the road, turned there toward Thornhill on the still distant northern coast and lengthened her stride into a ground-eating pace. In moments, she was out of sight.

Zero looked up into the rain-weeping skies and said, "Well, I'm committed now."

He walked back inside to dry himself off once again and care for the sick children. It would be a long night without Bessariel's company.

Sometime later, but still before midnight, he remembered his mother making carrot soup for a human neighbor's sick children. There was chilled milk in the cold cellar, gone a bit sour, but the cooking would help that, he thought. Plenty of carrots in one of the dry bins. He'd chased most of the chickens back to the barn, but one of the ones who'd refused eviction wasn't given time to regret it. Bannock watched him suspiciously but was won over at last with a pair of chicken legs to crunch.

Zero cleaned the bird, putting the feathers aside for later use, and got it started boiling down for stock. That done, he slipped outside to take more hot water to his ghoul and feed the other critters.

The ghoul gave him a guilty look when Zero came into the barn. He pointed to a wicker chicken 'to market' basket in which close to half a dozen small birds were now rattling about. "Are these something I can eat?" he asked, shivering.

"O sweet Gods, yes. Here, drink this first." Zero handed him the mug of hot water and the ghoul wrapped himself around it and began sucking it down.

"I'll set some foot snares," Zero told him. "You stay in here out of the wet. Some hares will warm you better than the birds."

"Are all the Risen like you and me?" asked the ghoul, more properly now, Zero realized, a fledgling necroknight.

"Free Undead," Zero corrected. "We are part of the Free Undead. The Risen Tsar doesn't have his hooks into you. Or me. Not any longer."

The blue flame in Zero's eye sockets turned more violet as he fell silent for a long moment before he spoke again to continue. "But yes. And no. The skeletons and zombies are mindless, but you can give them commands like you would a construct." At the younger knight's confused look, he added, "Like a golem or pieces-parts man."

"The bodiless," Zero continued, leaning back against the wood of a stall, "spectres, ghosts, and some less common others - they don't need to eat or drink, at least not solid food as the living and some undead do. They steal life and arcane energies from everything around them. Some of them can talk, if they choose." He frowned, adding, "Some of those can cast spells as they did when they were living. Some can even cast holy spells and those are the most dangerous to us of them all. All the bodiless are best avoided. They are almost impossible for any but the most powerful resurrectionists – you'd likely call them necromancers – or litches, or necroknights to control or persuade to do anything but what they themselves please."

"What about the ones more like us?" the younger knight asked, eying the birds in the wicker cage.

"Us. Hmm," Zero lifted a ragged eyebrow as he studied the newly undead human necroknight. "There are several possibilities with embodied, thinking undead.

The first are ghouls and necroknights like us. Both types can get some energy out of fresh, still growing plants but living meat animals – humans, elves, and the other kindred races included - are best when we need to feed to regenerate ourselves quickly. It's a lot safer to kill whatever you are going to eat first."

Zero paused a long moment, then continued reluctantly, but honestly, "You do get more energy if you eat them alive, but it does bad things to your mind. Kill them first and then eat. We don't actually need the meat, but it helps keep us warm. Don't waste your time on fish, snakes, or lizards unless the weather is extremely hot. Likewise, get too cold and you can't function, undead or not."

"Would it kill us? Again, I mean?"

"No, but if you're frozen solid, it *hurts* and anything can come along and eat you. Or chop off your head. Or light you on fire - All of those things *can* kill you. Likewise, don't stay underwater too long or you'll end up as fish food."

"So, what am I?" The young necroknight set aside his now empty mug and started eyeing up the caged birds again.

"See if you can grab a chicken," Zero suggested. He was sure he already knew what sort of undead he was teaching, but this would prove it.

The knight started to get up.

"No. Sit. Look at a chicken and think about pulling it to you. Gesture at it if you need to, but try it. They can't move faster than you anymore, if this doesn't work and you have to actually run one down."

The knight gave him a doubtful look, glanced around, and made a grabbing gesture at one of the closest hens - and dropped the startled bird in surprise when purplish tendrils of energy yanked it into his hands.

Then his hunger got the better of him and he fell upon the chicken before it could flee.

"Not bad for a first try," Zero said, watching him. "And you're definitely going to be a necroknight. We have magick. Ghouls are basically humans or elves or dwarves, just dead, so they're cold and grumpy all the time."

"Mmffpt!" replied the fledgling necroknight, spitting out a mouthful of feathers.

Zero continued, "The Risen you'll really need to watch out for are other necroknights, because they'll probably all be older and stronger than you. Vampires and leannan shee; I don't know if dwarves or giants have vampires, but they might. Don't know what they're called though or how their powers might be different than vampires or leannan. Liches. Liches are dead mages or priests who kept their magicks - nasty as a pudding full of knives. Demons – they aren't undead, but demons fuck up everything. And then there's the Risen Tsar."

Zero paused, not wanted to make a target of himself by even thinking too much about the Risen Tsar, much less speaking about him. "Just keep away from the Russ," he finally settled on. "And if you hear he's marching again, get the hell out of his way.

Then his mood changed and he added, "Unless you want to try to help the rest of us take him down? Him. Or Koshchey." Zerollen's eyes gleamed with a dangerous purple-blue light like a tiny thunderstorm. "Then maybe we'd be able to go on to whatever heaven or hell might be waiting for us."

"Do you think God would allow sinners like us into His Heaven?"

"I think my horse talks to me," said Zero with absolute conviction. "So, anything is possible. But I'm certainly no expert on what the humans' Nameless God might allow. You'd have to talk to one of the free necroknights or a ghoul who was a holy warrior in orders or a priest about that one." The storm in Zero's eyes had dispersed.

"Done with that?" he asked, and, "Feeling any better?"

"Maybe." The young necroknight handed Zero the chicken carcass – what was left of it. "It won't animate, will it?"

"Oh, good Gods, no!" Zerollen shuddered. "Undead chickens…. No! No one needs that. Besides, we don't pass on what we are, even by feeding like you just did. We have to make a conscious effort to pull someone back, unlike the vampires or leannan shee, and even they wouldn't turn a chicken. Mostly, even when we do, there isn't really anyone home. Just our bad luck you'd picked up the taint somewhere. I didn't mean to stick you with this, but if you ever fought undead, you could have gotten bitten or breathed in poisonous air..." Zero shrugged. "My animating your body was likely the tipping point, but you might have Risen on your own, given how quickly you're adapting."

"Well, if I was in Hell, I don't remember it, but that's where I'd probably have been. Or Limbo. So, maybe this is a chance to atone for what I did?"

"Maybe," said Zero. "Just remember, we can always fuck things up worse for ourselves, too."

They sat there for a few more minutes, listening to the patter of rain, and the occasional mutterings from the remaining chickens, the caged birds, or the horse or cow.

"I need to go set those snares and clean this," Zero finally said, giving the carcass a shake, "for more stock for the soup I'm making. I'll bring you something else warm to drink in a couple of hours."

"Why are you taking care of those kids anyway?" The young knight handed him the empty mug.

"Atonement of my own?" Zero shrugged. "I've done enough harm in the world. And I grew up in Tir na Scota and Scotland and the Debatable Lands. These were my people. Or close enough. Besides, I think their mother appeared and pointed me to them. If I don't come back out for you after two hours or so, come over to the house, it'll probably mean I'm too busy to bring you anything warm myself."

2: MEASLES AND AN OLD FRIEND

Sick children were messy. Zero hadn't had brothers and sisters of his own, but he'd helped his mother with enough of their human and half-blood neighbors to remember what needed done. Hector had recovered enough to be able to get himself to a chamberpot, but the two girls were in a bad way, though Aggie could give enough warning he could help her get to the pot most of the time. Somehow Zero was managing to juggle the necessities and cleanup along with dumping and rinsing out the chamberpots, cleaning himself off, and keeping up with getting water and broth into the children. He was even singing to them, in Elvish, an utter nonsense song he remembered his mother singing:

"Fish-flop, Fish-flop,
Living in the sea.
I caught a Fish-flop
And it came home with me.
Fish-flop, Fish-flop,
Swimming all around …"

But as he'd half-expected, Zero wasn't overly surprised to find the young knight come silently into the mud room and now standing there, staring at him as though he weren't certain the senior knight still had a mind.

"I never thought I'd live to – Never thought I'd ever hear a necroknight singing lullabyes to living children," said the man. "Or see one looking embarrassed to be caught at it."

Bannock grumbled suspiciously when he saw the knight but didn't bother to get up from where he was curled next to Hector. The knight looked over the restless children near the hearth with a wistful expression. "Home. But not mine," he said, accepting another mug of heated water from Zero.

He nodded at the blanket across the stairwell. "No one upstairs?"

"Just mice and sparrows in the eaves," Zero told him.

"We could hang the washed bedding up to dry in here or upstairs," suggested the knight. "I could check the upstairs rooms for leaks and string lines."

"Not to be rude," Zero told him, "but your control isn't the greatest right now and you're bigger than I am. I'd rather not have to fight you if you go for the dog or one of the children."

"I wouldn't –" The young necroknight stopped himself. Looking chagrined, he admitted, "No, you're probably right to be worried about me. I feel…like a drifting boat. If that makes any sense."

"More than I like to remember," Zerollen told him.

"I found a quiver of arrows and a bow hidden in the hay. I'll try hunting something once the rain stops. I think I remember animals will come out to feed then."

"They will. But don't wander more than a mile out. And if you're along the road, keep an eye out for any bodies - the children's father might be lying out there somewhere." Zero frowned at the thought, but added, "With any luck we'll have at least one hare in the snares by morning."

***

By first light the rain had stopped and they did have one hare to split between them. They also had a newborn calf, but neither of them had any wish to harm it. The new necroknight dressed himself in his mostly dried clothing and took the poacher's bow and arrows he'd found and began casting along the edges of the fields for more hares or a deer or stag. Zero returned to spooning the broth from the carrot soup he'd made into the children. He drank more water, as hot as he could tolerate without damaging his mouth or throat, but the carrots weren't fresh enough to give him any useful energy, so he kept the broth just for the children.

He took a break about mid-morning to check on the old horse and the cows. The wooly cow guarded her calf zealously from Zero, but he managed to get enough of a look to feel fairly certain she'd birthed another cow and not a baby bull. The old horse was eager for grain, which Zero sparingly shared out, not sure what reserves the farm had for a semi-starved plow horse who was looking more and more like he was an actual warmount every time Zero saw him. A quick check of the fields showed the new grass hadn't been flattened too badly by the rain and didn't seem likely to rot. He was less certain about what he thought might be turnips or some over-winter crop. Whatever the plants were, they seemed healthy and not too overgrown with weeds. Unless they were weeds themselves, given how early it was in the growing season.

His unintended squire came back dragging a hart and chanting a list of names to himself, "Francis, Frank, Frederick, Fred, Gabriel, Gabe, Gamaliel, Garrett, George, Geoffrey, Gideon, Giles, Gil -- Geoffrey?" He stopped. "Geoff? Geoffrey? Yes! Geoffrey! I was Geoffrey; I am Geoffrey!" His eyes actually lit up with arcane blue flame and he did a little jig of purest pleasure around the hart. "My name is Geoffrey!"

"Any more to it than that?" Zero asked, coming over to inspect the hart.

"Yes," said his squire, eyes flickering darker to purple for a moment, before he shook off the question's reminder of other things he remembered. "But better for my family if I don't use it. Doesn't the Risen Tsar rename most of his necroknights?"

"Yes, but I don't recommend following his example. You'd end up being Geoffrey the Georgian or something like that."

"Eh! No, I don't think so. That's terrible," Geoffrey agreed. He looked almost like a living man again, except for his eyes and the greenish tinge his once-blond hair had taken on.

"Well, you've taken a most warrantable stag," said Zero. "And regained your given name. Honor him for his gift and call yourself Geoffrey Hart. Or Hartsbane. It would make an appropriately punish name for a new necroknight."

"Hartsbane." Geoffrey considered it. "Better to be the hunter than the hunted. And it fits. If I'm not to go around slaughtering people, harts and fallow deer are going to be on the menu."

"Sometimes a sad truth," Zerollen agreed.

"Would you share your use name with me, master knight?" Geoffrey asked.

"You've been around the Shee before, haven't you? And, of course. And pardon I didn't think to do it sooner. Zerollen diGriz." Zero gave a slight inclination of his head which wasn't quite a nod or a bow. "My father was a Portuguese sailor who washed ashore in Tir na Scota and caught my mother's eye. The Risen Tsar, in his pretense to following modern science and alchemy, dubbed me Zero Degrees. Most of my friends call me Zero."

"And I should use -" the young necroknight cautiously began.

"Zero is fine."

***

Another day went by.

Hector began being able to help feed his sisters. The old warsteed seemed to be visibly putting on weight. Bannock ranged out to catch his own hares or mice and the snares provided several hares as well to keep the edge off the pair of necroknights' hunger once they'd drawn what they could from the deer Geoffrey had poached.

Bessariel remained gone. Zero wasn't particularly worried - Thornhill was still a considerable distance away, even for a warsteed able to slip in and out of the Faelands and travel without his weight. And if anyone was following her, she'd be even slower coming back.

But Mary-wee wasn't responding to the water and food as well as he liked. Aggie was into the worst of her fever. There wasn't much time to think of anything but caring for the girls, the critters, Geoffrey, and himself.

Days became jumbled together.

"Zero," said Geoffrey, coming in with an armload of peat for the fire and looking to his sire and young Hector just finishing getting the girls into dry clothes once again. "We can't keep doing this. They need a real healer. I can see… something like a fog in the air around them both, but I don't know how to make it go away.

They need more than we can give them if they're going to live."

"My sisters aren't going to die!" exclaimed Hector. "Sir Zero, there's a healer in Invercraig, that's where Da was going. Can't one of you go find him and bring help back? It's not that far, just a half dozen miles up the road."

"Well," began Zero.

"I'm Anglish," said Geoffrey. "Better if you go. I've got enough control now - I took a roe deer this morning. You can trust me with the children."

"I suppose you're both right. I probably won't be back until tonight, even if I leave now and can find the healer quickly."

"Couldn't you take the horse?" asked Hector.

Zero shook his head. "That warsteed's not mine to ride. He'd probably accept being a plowhorse, but he'd be more likely to take you or one of your sisters or Geoffrey as a rider than let me mount him. I'm already claimed by one. And warsteeds are particular."

Zero salted a mug of hot water and drank it all down, dressed in his armor and gear, then wrapped a tartan blanket over his head and layered his waxed riding cloak and hat over all. After exchanging a warrior's clasp with Geoffrey and wishing knight and boy luck, he set off into a light morning drizzle.

It would probably have been a quick gallop along the road to the next farm, no more than a couple hours' trot to Invercraig at most, but he was also searching for a man who might have been fevered and collapsed off the road trying to reach the nearest burn. Often, he paused and sent tendrils of his necromantic energies probing down man-sized game tunnels through the gorse and bracken, only to startle hares and, once, a badger

Thunder was rumbling over the mountains before he finally reached the nearest farm.

"Hullo the house!" he called warily from the farmyard.

"Hullo, sassenach. Stay where you're at. We've had enough of Anglish raiders."

"Not a raider. Not Anglish, either," said Zero, dropping into the Highland tongue. "I'm looking for a man missing from his steading. His children have the measles and he went out looking for help. I'm not sure how many days ago that was."

"That'd be MacLean's bairns? You came up from the south?"

"Yes. Bound for Thornhill, but the wee uns had no one to help them, so I sent my mount on home and stayed. Have you seen their da?"

"Aye, he dragged himself through here near a week ago, bound for the hedgemage's place in Invercraig. That they're not at the farm is a bad sign." The speaker seemed to have relaxed a trifle once Zero had shifted into Gàidhlig. "It would be a kindness if'n you could put a word in for us with the healer as well."

"Sickness here as well?" Zero asked, moving closer to the door.

"Aye, more than a bit," admitted the voice.

"We'd share a dram," said an older voice and an elderly human with a blanket thrown over his head tottered out into the rain. "But fer ridin' or walkin', ye'll do better with this."

He handed over a steaming mug of heated ale. "Herbs for strength and heat for warming a man's bones."

He peered through the rain at Zero and his old eyes widened, blinking against more than the drops of water.

"Or one of the seelie. A gud day to ya, laird. Or Sir Knight, as ye may be."

"No laird, I. Just a simple soldier trying to do what's right."

The old man smiled at his voice and a memory clearly surfaced from the change in his expression. "I remember a road agent who gave the divil to the Anglish down on the Borders. Zero diGriz and his mare, Black Bess. That'd be you, isn't it? Was that her who raced by on the road a few days ago? Couldn't be the same mare though, after so many years, could it?"

Zero shook his head. "Sadly, no. That fine lady has been gone beyond the Rainbow Bridge many a year. But the warsteed who companies me now is a wonder and bears the same call name. I wish she were here that you could meet her." He studied what he could see of the old human, trying to lay a younger face over the aged features.

"Well, old lad," the man continued, "You take the road north and stay on it 'bout four miles more to the crossroads at the bridge, just beyond is Invercraig. The hedgemage and midwife have a place up the side road from the public house. The fever's bad in my youngest. Be wary of the bridge, the winter was hard on it, an' we've not gotten new timbers in. With all this rain, the water will be roaring down the gorge today."

Zero handed the emptied mug back to his old human acquaintance.

"You get your own self back inside, Alasdair MacIver," he said, putting a name to the face aged almost beyond his memory. "I'll have a dram or two with you when I get back."

"Should we send someone down fer tha bairns?"

"If you can spare them. I left my squire to protect and help them. His call name is Geoffrey, tell him I sent you. But I'm planning to be back there tonight, though the Risen Tsar Himself try to bar my path."

Old Alasdair made a warding off gesture. "Go safe and swiftly, old friend. The water's rising in the heights."

Zero nodded and set off again.

3: THE ROAD TO INVERCRAIG

He moved a bit faster now, since it seemed less likely the children's father would have wandered far off the road. Or that if he had, he'd be beyond anything Zero would choose to do for him. Getting to the hedgemage's home seemed entirely the best choice for the children's survival. And then his trot brought him to the bridge. The bridge with the Craigburn now well beyond flood-stage pounding up and over its deck.

"Well, bugger it all!" he cursed. "That's not good." Even as he watched, a tree came tumbling through the water and lodged partway onto the bridge with a disturbing creak of outraged timbers. The whole structure shuddered and groaned as the water pivoted the tree, blocking half of the swift running stream and sending Zero backing away from the rising flood.

There was a path edged with light brush along the banks upstream, dangerously close to the swirling water rushing beside it, but he trusted it more than the splintering bridge half damming the flow. He sprinted up the path, bounding over rocks and rain-downed branches, dodging into the brush and small trees beside the trail when it disappeared under backwashes of ugly water. The path finally began climbing faster than the water and after a flatout run of better than an Anglish league, he was beginning to think about stopping and starting to look for a way across the peat-darkened flood.

That was the moment he put a foot wrong on a damp, slick stone and went tails over teacups into a patch of yellow whin brambles. Threatening damnation on all such plants, Zero fought his way out of the patch and continued, back at a walk, and picking prickles out of his trousers and other uncomfortable spots. He finally had to stop and shake out his boots before he was able to continue, now limping. He might be undead, but sharp wood, however small, could still cause discomfort.

A couple of hours later, now well off his schedule, he came across an old soldiers' road and another bridge spanning the river. Though in some disrepair, the old stone bridge, like the narrow road itself, was in better condition than the timber one he'd wanted to take. He gratefully crossed with a word of thanks to the memory of its builders.

Another path flanked the river on this side as well, somewhat wider and with better footing than the one Zero'd just traveled. He gave it a sour stare, then set off to recover the distance his detour had cost him. He found a downed branch he was able to turn into a walking stick with a few chops of his hand axe and a minor bit of carving with his boot knife. Still, it was afternoon with more than the rain clouds alone starting to darken the day before he reached the coastal road again. The bridge looked even more untrustworthy now with part of its decking carried away, but the water level had dropped back down once the tree had ripped its way through the blockage.

He tried picking up the pace since he was almost to Invercraig, but his leg only allowed him about three strides before his ankle turned again and dumped him full-length into a puddle he'd tried to jump.

He'd just settled against a low stone wall beside the road to dump water out of his boots when a gust of wind brought him the scent of wet horses and the sound of shod hooves on stones. Years of life and undeath as a hunted man and reluctant soldier sent a prickle of premonition sharp as the whin thorns through him. He jump-rolled over the crowning stones of the wall and sheltered tight against its length. Squirming on his stomach, he eeled his way along a rabbit run into a patch of brush and brambles and rose just enough to peer over the wall, squinting through the multitude of branches and thorny bramble canes to hide the arcane gleam of his eyes as much as possible. He was thankful his weather cloak and hat were of a muted grey-green-brown shade which blended in with the drab background, but then, he'd picked them with such occasions as this in mind.

Riders passed at a trot. Four humans in a motley of colors - mostly of Anglish military, though none of the same company - and equally motley armor and armed likewise with a mismatch of weapons which told Zero they were no laird's men. Yet they moved with more discipline than most of what passed as town milia these days could muster.

It seemed very likely they were the raiders - or some of the raiders - the MacLean children had told him about. He gave their retreating backs a long, thoughtful stare. He could take four normal soldiers or warriors, especially from surprise, but was it worth the risk of injury?

Before he could commit to any action against them, the snap and ring of more shod hooves warned him into cover again as a baker's half dozen more riders followed the first group. They didn't seem to be in pursuit, more likely part of the same band and a nasty surprise for anyone attacking the outriders.

"I wonder what they'll think of the bridge? Will they be foolish enough to try to cross it with horses?" Zero whispered to himself. It was no more than a good arrow's flight or perhaps two, away, just out of sight now behind a turn in the twisty coast road. "MacIver's farm should be safe enough, unless they ride most of what's left of the day - there's no quick way to take horses along the far side's path. And humans usually don't travel at night unless for war and raids, so the farms along the road may stay safe until tomorrow. Or the raiders could take the old war road instead and leave the southern farms alone. Or they could turn around and come right back."

He heard some shouting from the direction of the bridge, but it quickly fell silent again. When no more riders came from the direction he wanted to travel and the ones already passed didn't return, he dared start moving again.

"But will there be anything left of Invercraig when I get there?" he asked himself.

He kept tight to the wall and whatever other cover along it he could find, in case any more raiders approached from either direction. Wisely, because a lone rider appeared suddenly on the road, horse at an easy lope as they headed back toward the village. No more were visible behind the rider.

It was too good an opportunity to let pass.

He reached out with a hand and his will and pulled. His magick yanked the unprepared rider onto the road, the fall knocking the air from the rider's lungs in a great woosh and leaving him gasping long enough for Zero to dart out and drag him behind the wall. The blade of Zero's boot knife opened the raider's throat, while tendrils of arcane energy - black against the shadow of the wall - engulfed the shocked raider. Zero fed fully for the first time since he'd taken a deer days before discovering the sick MacLean children. The deer and other creatures he'd shared with Geoffrey had helped sustain him, but the dying man restored him to his full semblance of life, healing the damage to his foot and leg and pushing the painful chill of his undead existence away for at least a few hours.

No one else followed the rider.

The horse, feeling the sudden loss of its rider, had stopped and begun cropping grass along the verge of the wall not far away. Zero considered it while he disposed of his kill in the same way he had hidden from the raiders, tucking the body behind and tight against the stones, partially hidden under the very brush he'd been lurking in.

He made soothing noises to the chestnut horse as he slowly worked his way closer, carefully not looking directly at it. Though it shuffled uncertainly, he was able to grab a rein when the animal stepped on the same and soothe it out of bolting. By leading it near the wall, he was able to mount without too much difficulty, and ride the rest of the way to where he could peer through the mist at Invercraig.

The village, what little he could see of it, was still standing. There was no scent suggesting any large fire had been or was burning nearby, removing one worry.

A guard in the same sort of mismatched garb as the raiders Zero had already seen loitered just beyond a short span of stone culvert over a millrace which paralleled the low village wall. "What's brought you back so quick?" the man grumbled, starting to pull himself upright to block the gap in the wall he was apparently supposed to be guarding as Zero urged his mount closer.

"Bridge's out," Zero told him with a certain bloodthirsty glee, coming right alongside the raider. He brought his hand axe down on the man's head and followed him to the ground, making sure the raider would never rise again. "And now, so are you."

His commandeered mount, as supremely unconcerned with its new rider's sudden departure from its back as it had been with the original, dropped its head and began cropping the grass along the millrace, while Zero arranged the man as though he'd gone to sleep against the wall. Leaving the horse to graze for the moment, he studied the village. Even with the fog starting to roil up from both mountain and sea, the cottages seemed noticeably dark and still. He only saw a hint of smoke, barely distinguishable from the mist, when all the chimneys should have been sending their own peaty clouds to mingle with the salt-scented air.

"Dead?" he asked himself. But the buildings hadn't been fired, if that were the case. There wasn't the oppressive feeling of angry spirits still lingering, not even from the human he'd just slain. Still, people should be moving around in the afternoon. Zero shifted several of his smaller weapons and shook the blanket from under his riding cloak. He draped it around the dead man, covering the head wound and hiding most of the blood. He wished he had a bottle to leave as further distraction from the dark stains he couldn't cover. But no blood had run down the corpse's face, so in the dimming light he might be mistaken for falling asleep at his post until morning or whenever his replacement showed up to take his place.

Feeling better able to fight if he needed to, Zero walked through the gap in the wall and into the village. His original assessment of the place being unnaturally still was not improved upon once he was inside the low wall. The High Road was empty. So were the yards he glimpsed down walkways between buildings which didn't share a common wall. He knew he'd passed through Invercraig more times than he remembered, but nothing had ever happened here to make a lasting memory other than the tavern sign where a rather impressively realistic salmon protruded out of a wavering blue circle apparently intended to represent water and opened its mouth to catch, not an acorn of wisdom, but an ale-shaded arc from a blob Zero thought was either intended to be a mug or perhaps, a small keg.

The Drunken Fish had light in its small windows, though the lantern hook on its sign was absent. A lantern did glow through the thickening fog down a side road just beyond the mill, marking the stables where Zero remembered being told post horses were kept. None of the small shops along the High Road bore lanterns or lit windows, but as Zero stepped careful along their fronts, a faint glow appeared around the corner of the last building before a side street broke the line of houses before the tavern.

Peering cautiously around the corner, he saw the second building up the side road was a free-standing stone and plaster house with a covered porch and a horse rail just off the lane. A warmly glowing mage-lit sign showing a mortar and pestle over a staff still bearing leaves at its head and a snake which twined its way up the staff and through the carved leaves. Faint behind thick curtains, the ground floor windows dimly glowed as well.

The click of shod hooves warned him the horse he'd claimed was on the move and he ran back to intercept it before it turned down the mill road to the stable and alerted anyone who might be there.

Leading the horse, Zero retraced his steps and tied the placid creature to the horse rail outside the healer's home. Pushing his weather cloak back off his shoulders, he walked up to the door and knocked.

Faintly, at the edge of his hearing, he caught voices. They rose quickly, but indistinctly, then a 'be right there' came, still muffled but definitely closer.

The door opened with the silence of well-made and well-oiled hinges, letting out the smell of herbs, fried fish, and an underlaying scent of illness.

A tall, sharp featured woman peered out at him. "What is it this -? Oh!" She clearly hadn't been expecting a necroknight at her door.

They stared at each other for a moment, before the woman visibly gathered herself and asked, "Yes? What need brings you here?"

"Sick children, good healer."

She blinked at that. "I can't - "

"They have measles," Zero pressed quickly. "One seems to be shaking it off, but two others are worsening, perhaps something else getting a hold on them. And another farm I passed where they have the sickness as well ask I carry the message to you."

Her eyes darted toward the half-opened door, then back to him, "I've a houseful of sick here as well and can't leave. I'm sorry."

She started to shut the door - highly unusual for a herbwife, even faced with one of the dead walking.

Zero gave her a raised eyebrow and shifted to let her glimpse his sword belt, which could be taken as warning or promise of aid, depending on how she interpreted it.

She bit her lower lip, glanced at the door again, and said, "I can make you up a powder to mix with whisky. It should help. You should wait here." She made as if to shut the door again.

"I've been tending the sick for near a sevenday myself, and I'm not sick yet," Zero told her with a wry grin. "I doubt it'll bother me to wait inside out of the cold. And I give you my word, I'll do *you* no harm."

She nodded ever so slightly at his emphasis. "On your head be it then," she said and stepped back and away from the door, gesturing for him to come in, "As ye do not harm to me and mine, be welcome in my home."

Zero nodded a half-bow and nimbly stepped inside, feeling the threshold energies parting to let him through. They couldn't have stopped him if he'd pushed his way in, but they would have hurt him, how badly he wasn't certain. But there was real power there.

Even granted entrance, the protection on the healer's home slowed his reactions just enough and though he was certain trouble waited behind the door, he wasn't able to completely dodge the sudden strike from the hidden raider.

Zero didn't quite black out; he could hear the resumption of arguing between the outraged healer and her guard. The raider had made the mistake of thinking he was done and the herbwife was doing an excellent job of distracting the man and luring him partway into the hall, turning his back to the fallen necroknight.

Zero got silently to his feet, wincing a bit at the bright lights flickering across his vision. The sight of the cast-iron skillet he'd been hit with only increased the necroknight's annoyance at being blooded by a mortal.

"That really wasn't very smart of you," said Zero, spinning the man around, seizing his arm, and driving the skillet up into his jaw, snapping his head back. He felt the bone give in the human's face and followed the move with a thrust to the throat.

Choking and gagging, the man dropped to his knees, clawing at his crushed neck.

"Sorry about the blood on your walls," Zero said, still holding the skillet in case anyone else attacked.

The herbwife surprised him by spitting on the dying man. "That one I'll not regret putting on the pyre," she said with some heat. She made a visible gathering of her control, smoothing her sleeves before speaking again in a calmer voice.

"So, elf knight, can you be helping us?" she asked, politely ignoring his undead status. "There's more of them."

"Here?" Zero asked in turn.

The woman shook her head, "Not in the house, not ones as can do any harm, but they're scattered all over the village." She pushed passed Zero to close and bar the door. "But they have most of those they didn't kill at first mewed up in the tavern. And they hold our children on the good behavior of the rest of us."

Zero growled softly, "Where?"

"Somewhere up in the ruins of the great house on the crag."

"I saw eleven ride out to the south, but the bridge is too damaged to take horses across right now. Ten of them took the path along the burn, unless they're trying to fix the bridge."

"You said there were eleven?"

"One of them started back here." Zero showed his teeth. "I helped him off his horse."

"I take it he won't be bothering anyone else either?"

"I'd feel more certain on it once I'm seeing him on a pyre, but nothing suggested he'd be standing up again."

"Well then, come with me. I'll get you out the back, where no one's like to see you in this fog. Leave the horse. If any of them see it, they'll think its rider came to me for some reason and I can put them off with some story of him taking ill. The way they've been dropping, it'll be believed. If they hadn't taken the children, we'd have turned on them before now."

She stopped and gave Zero a hard look. "You wouldn't know anything about why the lot of them are ill, would you?"

"I'm just a courier for the Protestant Union, goodwoman healer. If a ghost hadn't turned me toward the children I've been caring for, I'd have ridden in here blind and either been passed through or ambushed days ago by this troop of raiders. How many are still on their feet and can fight?"

"Was there a guard at the gate?" she asked him in turn.

"There *was*."

"I see you're efficient. And informed."

"Old Alasdair MacIver and his kin warned me they'd been ranging. I've never liked the Anglish much and I like forager-requisitioners who prey on their own even less."

"Good man. Elf." She corrected herself, flustered. "Knight."

"Seelie," Zero corrected her. "At least, as much as I can be and be what I am now."

They'd already crossed the house to the kitchen door. "Here," she said. "Take this."

She pulled a small pottery jar sealed with wax off a shelf and pushed it into his hand, while pulling the bloody skillet from him. She put it into her sink and pulled down a bottle from an open cabinet. "What's in the jar is for you. Give this," she held up the bottle, "to the village children if you manage to save them. It will strengthen them and calm their fears, but only for a limited time. Tell them Goody Greneglais said all of them were to have a sip."

She pulled down several folded and waxed packets as well. "This is for your foundlings and the MacIvers. Give it to Molly MacIver and she can mix it up for you. In case I don't make it through the excitement you've started.

"There's fewer than a dozen left, but I don't know where all of them are. At least one on the north gate and a couple at the stable. One lurking somewhere watching our boats, so no one steals out to sea. Some keeping most of the town in the tavern."

"Thank you. I'll try for the children first."

"Thank you, for doing what you're doing. Bright Lady Mary and your Gods protect you," she told him.

Her backdoor led into an herb garden or what would be one once the rains turned warmer. Zero hurried along the paths between the planting beds. Fog had filtered in through her vine-woven fence, but not so heavily as out on the lane. The healer's yard light was dimmed to a golden orb through the mist, the windows faint blurs. The Drunken Fish was hidden in the grey-white cloud, only emerging as he picked his way across the lane and closer to it. He took the alley behind the tavern, keeping to the footpath which ran along the jakes and the shed where travelers might tether their mounts, then along the back fences of the houses and shops fronting on the High Road. He startled a hare and a few small birds and encountered one supremely disinterested ginger cat perched on a wall like a loaf set to cool. If there were any watchers other than the animals, he saw none and no one raised the hue and cry in his passing. A chained hound bared fangs in a warning snarl from inside the open gate to an uphill garden, but thankfully didn't break into a clamor of barking as Zero edged by on the far side of the footpath. And then he was to another lane, this one leading down to the High Road again.

The guard here had a sentry box to stand in and Zero almost missed him in the ground-hugging cloud blanketing Invercraig.

"Here you are," the guard said, stepping out of his box and stretching. "What's the word?"

"Bollocks!" said Zero, jumping sideways and yanking the man off balance. He put his small knife across the man's throat before he could let out a yell and dragged him outside the town's northern gate and off the road into the inevitable bramble of yellow whin. In disgust at the mass of prickles, Zero pulled off the blanket the man had had thrown over his shoulders for a cloak and wiped off as many of the stickers and as much of the blood as he could. He left the body in the whin and the blanket rolled and tucked behind the resumption of the low wall bordering the High Road as it left off being the village High Street and fully turned into the coastal road again. He'd have rather burnt the blanket for the traces of his own blood drawn by the accursed whin that might have been on it, but he suspected he was running out of time before the sentries were due to change.

4: CRAIG HOUSE

The lane leading up to the Great House of Invercraig parted from the coastal road just outside the village and switch-backed up the crag. The road was old and well built, with culverts diverting the water which might otherwise have returned the way to so much rocky hillside. The road rose above the cloud layer, leaving the old stone gleaming damply in watery afternoon sunlight. Below, the village and much of the coast was still covered in a thick layer of fog.

"Really?" Zero asked of his surroundings, but nothing was so bold as to reply. "Well, there's not but doing it anyway."

He squared his shoulders and continued up the road as though he owned the place.

The stone walls which had once slowed attackers were mostly down to the ground. Some still lay where they had fallen, other sections gone, perhaps carried off for building in the village below. The cobbles of the way were still firmly set, even interspersed with bands of the underlying stone. And the Great House stood mostly intact, part of the roof burned away, windows on the upper levels gaping, but it was possible they'd never been glazed at all.

No one showed themselves at the grand entrance where the crest of the old laird's family still graced the stone above the lintel. Zero walked up, alert for movement, preternatural senses probing ahead for life. Cold stone, damp, old burnt wood, overlaid with the fresh and pungent scent of burning peat, were the chief smells. No scents or sounds suggested any living being, nor any embodied spirits lurking near the doorway, but remembering his painful encounter at the healer's home, Zero probed the dark within with seeking tendrils of his own arcane energies.

Confirming nothing living nor undead was in the immediate area, he ducked and rushed inside, moving as far from the doorway as the heaviest shadows would allow. Neither arrows nor bolts followed his movement.

Eyes adjusting to the dim light, he scanned the shadows of the hall, noting the dark openings of several archways and what seemed likely to be a stairwell. The far end of the hall was hidden by the relative blaze of sunlight through the doorway and a second spill of light from a loophole which should have commanded access to the house. A glow of embers marked a fireplace midway down the hall. Between the sunlight and the smoldering fire, the deeper shadows beyond could have hidden any number of foes, but the lack of response to his hurried arrival suggested no one shared the room with him.

A narrow door offset from the entrance was just barely visible now, closed or mostly so. A faint flow of air came from somewhere above him. Wide stairs, well-broader than the door he could now see, led in the direction of the air flow. He took those stairs up to a landing where a tapestry or other hanging blocked what was likely another loophole and most of the light it would have let in. Stairs led both up and down into some other area from the landing. Both ways seemed equally dark.

He started up, moving with the caution of the highwayman and sneak thief he had once been. Six steps and the stairs turned sharply to the left and toward better lighting again. He stopped and felt in a belt pouch for the square shape of a polished bit of metal he'd taken from a Polish nobleman during one of continuous card games played aboard ship while the Protestant Union had been either pursuing or retreating from the Risen Tsar's armies. Holding the mirrored square low, he angled it around the corner and up, hoping he'd guessed right and the guard the raiders had on the town's children would be waiting for him here.

He caught a glimpse of a dark shape crouched at the top of the stairs just before a bolt ripped the mirror out of his hand.

Crossbows took forever to be redrawn. Zero charged up the dozen stairs and had just reached the landing when the crouched figure brought up a second crossbow and calmly fired right into his guts. Zero's eyes squished shut with the pain as his body instinctively tried to curl around the wound, but he managed to blindly bring his handaxe down on the weapon. Which was helpful, but he'd been aiming for the human's head. He used his momentum to follow the need to curl up and rolled to a hard stop against the hallway wall, but back on his feet again.

The raider clouted him on the head with their mangled crossbow and pelted down the corridor, but instead of making for the tower stairwell at the far end, they jinked around a corner and out of sight before Zero was able to take two steps after them.

A bolt in the guts would put many fighters down. It didn't do much to a necroknight beyond causing them a great deal of pain, unless it lodged in a hip or took out the spine. Zero snarled and forced himself fully upright, mentally cursing the holes through his leathers and his body, now leaking his thin, watery blood out both sides before the wounds could draw shut. The warning purple glow of his arcane death magicks roiled like smoke around him as his control wavered, but he ignored them and threw himself into pursuit, leaping high and wide as he came to the corner.

A third bolt flew under his feet and cracked into the wall behind him as he landed and finally got a look at who he was fighting. His main impression was they were damn big to be so fast, and barely succeeded in using his tendrils to yank yet another crossbow away from the raider before they could grab it. "How many of these damned things do you have?" Zero demanded, reversing the weapon and loosing a bolt back at the rapidly retreating human. But the raider skidded around yet another corner, though Zero thought the bolt had at least scraped their back in passing.

"Stop! You idiot!" commanded a voice with enough power behind it to bring Zero to a sudden, furious halt. "Before you get yourself killed."

The specter of a human knight marred with its own death wounds had manifested in front of him. "Again," it added drily, returning Zero's glare with one of its own. "I'd ask what you're doing galloping though my halls, but we'll save that for later. There are children to be rescued and you, sir, are going the wrong way."

"What?" barked Zero, thoroughly confused and bringing up his sword.

"Oh, stop that, fool. Take the tower stairs up to the landing. I'll delay the jackanapes, but you must hurry. Go!"

The specter disappeared, leaving Zero to retrace his path as quickly as he could. That was part of the fun of being a necroknight, he thought, having strange undead just ordering you about whenever they felt like it. But Zero wasn't eager to dispute orders with a ghost, not when their goal seemed the same.

The stairs were steep and narrow, but no longer constrained by needing to be quiet, Zero raced up them and out into a hall almost identical to the one below it, but for openings to narrow balconies abutting on the tower and the carefully arranged crossbows on the floor. There was also a door made instantly noticeable by recent repairs and oiled hinges. There was no connection at the far end of the hall to the stairwell Zero had followed up from the grand entrance room, just a built-in stone seat and a wider arrow loop. But a side corridor did match approximately the location of the one below it though with a greater glow of natural light than he would have expected of an interior hall, until he remembered the damaged roofline he'd seen on his way in.

"You can't have them," came a voice from that hall, shrill and edged with madness. "They're mine! Mine to gut and flay and furrow as I please. Mine forever!"

The crossbow man came backing into sight, swinging a silvery butcher knife warningly with one hand, and with yet another small crossbow clutched to his body in the other.

The specter of the knight followed, but warily, seeming to have more caution of the madman's blade than Zero would have expected from one of the bodiless.

Then Zero noticed the steady drip of essence running down one of the spectral knight's arms and onto the floor and realized the butcher knife wasn't silvery, but glowing with its own light.

The madman had somehow infused the blade with his own lifeforce, in effect making it just as deadly to the specter and to Zero himself as if it had been blessed by a true holy believer. And the madman knew it. "Kill you dead, ghostie man," he warned the specter, slashing at it again with alarming swiftness.

Catching sight of Zero, he started toward him, "Kill you too, elf man. Make you bleed, gut you like I'll gut me them little uns, once you're dead."

But Zero had something the specter didn't have and the madman couldn't use one handed. He had the crossbows, already winched back and bolts nocked.

"How about we see how you like being gutted, you crazy git," he said and put a bolt into and through the mad raider.

The terrifying thing about the truly mad was, like the undead themselves, it often took a mortal blow to put them down. And even dying, they could still be deadly.

The raider screamed and charged Zero, stabbing at anything he could reach. He was taller than the necroknight and outweighed him. Both went down in a pile on the floor, the raider stabbing, Zero doing likewise with his boot knife until the pain of the perversely holy weapon broke through the veil of his humanity and released the killer the Risen Tsar had made of him. With the scream of a broken soul, Zero unleashed the dark arcane power within him, throwing the larger human halfway down the hall. Zero staggered after him, stomping on his hands as he attempted to grab his obscenity of a holy knife again before tearing open the madman's gambeson, and then the bloody wound the bolt had left. And then Zero fed.

"Tell me, knight," came a powerful voice through the already fading haze of warmth, "are you a man again or just another ravening beast to be put down?"

Zero snarled in reply, turning toward the voice. It commanded, but not with the power of that other he dimly remembered. Remembered enough to know he would never submit to being used so again.

A ghostly knight met his glare and rising fury. And in the way of ghosts, it shared its own memories of the last moments of its mortal life with him and those of its death. And Zero remembered being in a place like this before, remembered being part of the horde thrown at those walls and desperately barred doors. Remembered the killing and fell to his knees as memory and still mortal conscience wracked him with the terrible guilt.

"I ask again," said the specter. "Are you a man? Have you a mind left?"

"Close enough to know you have brought me back to myself, specter. Everything hurts, so I must be back. Or as close to it as I can get anymore. What did I do this time? I didn't hurt the children, did I?"

"No, fool. Do you think I'd let you rise again if you'd even gone for them?"

"I'd hope not," Zero replied. He got a knee up and was able to push off the floor and stand again, though he staggered against a wall and almost fell as the impact sent an explosion of burning pain all though his sword arm and chest. "That knife—"

"Is where it will harm neither you nor I nor any innocents again. Or at least buried until someone is mad enough to go digging though the old cesspit to find the unholy thing." Zero had never seen a specter shudder before. It was disturbing and odd.

"Can you walk?" the specter continued, Zero's rattled memory finally recognizing this was the undead laird of Craig House who had aided him during the fight with the mad human. "We still need to get these children out of their prison and hidden elsewhere before any more of those curs come befouling my home again."

Zero considered the specter's words, tested them. "Yes," he said. "I can walk. Not well and not quickly, but I can walk. I'm just not sure I can be trusted around the living right now."

"You're a necroknight. Don't you know or carry anything to counter the harm an impowered weapon can do to you?"

Zero snorted. "I wasn't that important. Or powerful. Not when I was bound to the Risen. I just had the misfortune to be noticed and singled out by an old *friend*." The last word was heavy with sarcasm, but it reminded him of something.

"Invercraig's healer did give me a gift. Perhaps it might help. If it didn't get smashed in the fighting." He checked the pockets tied into his clothing. Amazingly enough, the packets, bottle, and wax-sealed jar were all still there and all intact.

He clumsily broke the seal with his off hand and more carefully wiggled loose the stopper.

"Ah!" sighed the specter, coming closer as a scent best described as clean and deeply green wafted out. It reminded Zero of the fresh cut cularan his mother would prepare for pickling and of thawing spring fields. The ointment within the jar was the palest of green in color as well. He struggled out of his cloak and enough of his gear to bare his torso and shoulder, the effort sending dazzling spears and explosions of light across his vision and making him grind his teeth against the pain.

More than a bit suspiciously - for anything smelling so strongly of the growing earth might burn him as badly as had that warped holy blade - he dabbed a finger onto just the surface of the ointment. When nothing unfortunate happened, he brushed it lightly over one of his chest wounds.

It felt as though he'd touched himself with cold green fire.

But when he could see once again that wound had closed, leaving behind a silvery scar which deepened to a vivid grass green against the faded brown of his once dark skin. Urged on by the specter, he got enough of the ointment into the unholy blade-caused wounds to regain movement and return some strength to his arm. He was also able to plug the hole in his gut, but couldn't reach far enough around his back to get the ointment into the exit wound there.

"There's not time to do more," the specter told him. "I'm feeling a stirring in Invercraig. We need to get the children moved."

There had been times when Zero had regretted his mortal life outside the law, certainly the guilt he felt for having been used as a killing puppet by the Risen Tsar haunted him. But he had no regrets about this most recent death he had caused, nor the skills he'd learned in his lawless youth to search bodies for the smallest of items.

Searching through what little remained of the madman's body, he found a brass key which opened the locked door. Inside what had been a bedroom, close to a score of human children stared back at him and the spectral knight with huge eyes and frightened expressions, until one of the older girls said, "Well, it's not Crazy Timothy who won the fight. What worse can they do than he wouldn't have?"

"I'm not here to hurt you," Zero assured them. "I know I must look like Death Itself right now, but your Goody Greneglais sent me to get you out."

"And that's the old laird," said one of the boys, pointing over Zero's shoulder to the specter. "Told you he was still here."

Zero took out the bottle and offered it to the closest child. "Healer Greneglais sent this for you. She told me all of you were to have a sip, so share it around. After what she did for me, I think whatever it is will help you as well. Is anyone injured? Anyone hurt?"

"Crazy Tim smacked us around some, but we've had worse beatings from our folks," said another of the boys.

"Then grab anything you need to take with you, get a sip of that distillation, and let's be going, young ones," the specter ordered.

After sharing crossbows out among the older children who'd had some experience with hunting or at least fishing, Zero led the children down the tower stairs. The specter of the laird kept disappearing and reappearing as they made their escape, offering reassurances none of the raiders were approaching the house. Instead of fleeing out the doors, the laird directed them across the grand hall to the stairwell Zero had originally climbed, but urged them downward this time, showing them the way through the servants' level to the wine cellar.

"I'm afraid the villains' master has claimed the steward's key to keep them from the drink, but I find myself hoping your rumored skill with locks had some foundation in truth, Sir Knight? If not, I'm afraid we might have to risk hiding the children somewhere else until the town is purged."

"You're not planning on keeping them in with the brandies, are you?" While iron bars might keep the raiders from the children as well as the casks of brandy francais, they'd do nothing to block bolts or arrows.

"I'm dead, not daft," grumbled the laird. "This is where my own four times over grandfather had the dwarves build an escape tunnel. It is still passable and one path leads right into Invercraig."

Zero blinked. "Well, if dwarves crafted the lock, that might be beyond me, but I'm willing to try my hand at it."

He rummaged into the bottom of one of his pockets, withdrawing several keys and several oddly-tipped bits of what might have been flattened nails or key blanks. He tried the keys in the lock first before switching to the odd flat bits, ending up with three of them wedged into the lock before the lock clicked open. Several of the children had pressed close to watch, one of the girls observing, "I think I could make those at the forge. When we get out of here, could I make tracings of them? Or wax impressions?"

Zero gave her a side-eyed look, "I suppose. Once things are safe."

The girl chewed her lower lip. "Right. Can I borrow them while we walk?"

She pulled a thin hook from somewhere in her clothing, twisted it in half, revealing what looked like an awl before she reattached the cover piece to the other end of the tiny awl. She held out a hand, "Please?"

Bemused by the display, Zero handed her one of his picks. "Whatever you're doing, I hope you can do it while we walk. And try not to lose that."

"I won't," she promised.

"Can we go now?" one of the other children asked.

Zero turned to where the laird was hovering in one corner of the wine cellar, "Push here and here. And down here with your toe," the specter told him.

The spots the old laird pointed out seemed no different from the rest of the stones, all hard to see in the deep shadows, and set low to the floor. "Now what?" Zero asked, when nothing happened.

"Push them all at once."

Zero yelped in pain and surprise as blades sheared through the tips of his fingers and took part of the toe off his boot. He jumped back, nearly tripped on the curious children, and ended up sprawled against a butt of brandy.

"Move away from him, children!" ordered the spectral laird. The children ducked out of sight around the barrels as Zero expounded on the nature of the trap builders and their likely lineages.

"Are you going to be able to control yourself?"

"Leave. Me. Alone!" Gasped Zero, more for needing the air to speak than really needing it, fumbling painfully for the green ointment again. The cool green scent steadied him by itself. He was able to put the little pot away again without actually having to use the cream inside.

After a moment, Zero continued, as his fingertips regrew. "I think so. But I'm not sure I'll be able to open your door. Dwarves really don't like undead. Especially undead trying to get into their secret places."

"I got it open," said one of the smaller girls. "See?" She waved excitedly at the now open gap in the stones.

"Are your hands -"

"I'm okay, Sir Knight. It didn't cut me."

"I got your bits," piped one of the others, while the other children filed into a dimly lit room through the opening in the wall. She shyly offered him his fingertips. "Do you need the piece of boot?"

"Just drop them in my hand, child. Don't touch me, if you can help it. I don't need the chunk of boot. The blade missed my toes."

"Probably shouldn't leave it here," said the girl and stuck it into one of her pockets.

The room beyond proved to be a landing at the top of wide, shallow stairs. Dim red light marked the stairs, leading down between still rough, but solid walls, the ceiling arched far enough above them a tall human male or female could have swung a claymore overhand. An obvious lever closed the door behind them.

"No more traps?" asked Zero.

"We'd sent our own out before the Risen's last attack, but they'd left the way open for us, if we could have taken it." The spectral laird gestured at the ceiling. "You saw how that worked."

"Before we go any further," Zero asked, "is everyone here?"

"All here, Sir," the children told him after a moment of counting and name calling.

Zero took the lead, moving carefully in the red light, but the wide stairs continued straight and downward without any blades flashing out of the walls or pits opening at his feet. Even when he drew his blade to add its own cold light to brighten the staircase, nothing designed to smite undead occurred. After an easy walk, he thought he saw another landing ahead.

Here the staircase split, the red-lit way curving to the left, while another stairway came suddenly into view, lit with a more orange light as he arrived at the landing. This stair was finer worked, but narrower. One fighter could have held it, provided they had a thrusting weapon.

"Stay left, on the red path," called the specter. "The other way, as long as you follow the orange light, will lead you to an exit several miles up the coast, but there's likely not much in the way of shelter there until you reach the old shrine to Nyorth. I should go no further, but the red stair leads down to the graveyard in Invercraig and a crypt for the families who served mine. There is a lever similar to the one at the top of the stairs which will open the wall. Another one inside the crypt will open the outer door, no doubt to the great consternation of anyone nearby, if they happen to see it. Godspeed to you and keep the children safe."

Zero sketched a salute to the laird and took the red stairs down with the same caution as he had started down the first section. It would serve him right, he thought, if he grew careless, for anything built by dwarves might react to him in a manner similar to the trap on the hidden passage's door, and graveyards were always chancy places for necroknights. But the stairs remained lit and solid, though the children reported the light had gradually gone out behind them on the stairs above the landing.

Before long he was standing at the end of the stairs. "Wait where you are, until I make sure the way is clear," Zero ordered the children. They had stopped crowding him once he'd drawn his blade and first heard the hum of the weapon. Now they sat down on the stairs to wait.

"I've been in battles with soldiers who didn't have the good sense you do," he told them. "If you hear fighting, don't wait to see if I win, run for the orange stairs as fast as you can and take them to the exit the laird told us about."

"Couldn't we stay with the laird?"

"Ah." That he hadn't expected. "You'd rather stay with one of the dead?"

"Pardon, Sir, but he's our dead," said the scruffy boy who Zero recognized as the one who'd turned to the others with the 'told you he was here' comment. "He's kin and he'll take care of us."

"Okay, then." Zero eyed the lever. "Ask him. He'll probably tell you the same thing, but the great house likely isn't safe for you to stay in long. But I remember being your age; you'll do what you'll do once I'm out of sight. Try not to get yourselves killed and I'll try to save your folks."

He pulled the lever and watched with wary interest as stair risers slid out from one of the walls and made a path up to where part of the ceiling opened. The opening let down a draft of colder air from the crypt above, but nothing else. He touched the blade of his sword and the hum and light ceased, leaving only the red glow from the stones. With some misgivings about how the children might react, he extended his senses, probing the area above for living or undead energies. Beyond a sudden collective gasp as his seeking tendrils became darkly visible around him, the children didn't make a sound. Nor did sounds come from the room above. Zero detected nothing living or undead. Curbing his eagerness to get out of another area likely containing dwarven created traps, he drew on his years as a sneak and scout to move silently up the steps into the crypt.

5: THE BATTLE OF THE DRUNKEN FISH

It was dark and quiet. Not even a rat still nested in the building. Still, Zero could smell old urine. If he pushed his vision, he could also see the faintest of glows along the areas where the rats had most often run and nested. He found the door by the strengthening of the drafts of air now sucking down into the tunnel. A bit of feeling around on the walls beside the door found the lever the laird had mentioned.

It opened, not the actual door, but a panel of what had seemed individual blocks of polished granite. Muted light, fresh salty air, and fog rolled in and Zero slid out, quietly as the stone.

No living humans seemed to be in the yard, though it stretched out of sight in the still heavy mist. More modest stone tombs and raised graves were thick between where he stood and the dark suggestion of the church.

The fog was thinner than when he'd first entered the village, but still enough to give him cover. He took to the back yards, flitting between outhouses and sheds, rabbit hutches and chicken coops, a small barn and paddock where a pair of wooly coos and a tiny isle pony as shaggy as a coo watched him with suspicious curiosity. At last, he found the healer's woven hedge and her back gate.

He snuck through her yard, listening, sniffing the air, watching through the thinning and thickening mists.

Small birds flitted about among the herb beds. Hens complained from the fenced and netted area around their coop. Several cats scattered from where they had been dozing in a clump near the back door. Zero wasn't anxious to catch any more crossbow bolts, nor even another frying pan, so he probed the room beyond the door, before letting himself inside.

The house was very quiet.

And the air was thick with the scent of emptied bowels and decay. And fresh blood.

He heard footsteps coming his way and took cover against the side of a cupboard.

Healer Greneglais came into the kitchen. Her face was tired and her posture slumped as she made her way to the hearth and swung the kettle out to pour heated water into a round dark brown teapot decorated with a pair of glazed blue lines.

"You needn't lurk there. I heard you come in. Come and warm yourself and tell me what you've done."

"If you'll do the same," Zero said, taking a seat across from her at her tiny table. "And thank you for your gift earlier. It helped me push back the madness and save the children.

She studied his face as he told her about the rescue.

"Thank you," she said as he finished. And she surprised him by catching up one of his hands and giving it a gentle kiss. "It makes what I did that much easier to bear."

"Tell me," he prompted.

"I killed them," she said, speaking of the sick raiders who'd been under her care, "and made sure they wouldn't Rise immediately, if they are going to; though they still need burned."

"Oh! Milady Healer!" he said in sympathy, knowing how thoroughly against all her training that had to have been.

Tears started, but she squeezed his hand fiercely and continued, even if there were catches between her words. "The ones who remain are stirred up and looking for you. I knew after they'd been here to warn their guard, I would have no better time. At least, with most of those stricken I'd had no hope they'd recover. That doesn't excuse it, but it makes it a little more bearable."

She drew herself up, wiped the tears away, and poured them both cups of a strong herbal concoction which smelled of bergamot and rose. "Now, we need to plan before the children get antsy and come out of hiding. The raiders are deflected from searching here for now, but that won't last beyond supper time, when their man and I don't go to the Salmon."

"Unless he does," Zero suggested. "We weren't that far apart in height and build. It would let me get inside, if I disguised myself as him."

"We could do that. You kill the raiders holding the parents. I'll free my friends and keep them from attacking you. And then we'll settle with the last few in the village." She took a drink and added, "His weather cape is in the hall close. I think his hat as well, but if not I've plenty more. What happened to yours?"

"Lost it somewhere along the way. Probably in one of those damned whin bushes on the edge of town."

"That might be for the good. If they found it outside of Invercraig, they might think you a traveler who continued on the road. They might still be out hunting for you in that case." She finished her drink and stood up, starting to fill her pockets with various pots and jars. "What shall we tell them? Since we shouldn't wait for supper time."

"Why not the truth?" Zero pitched his voice in a reasonable imitation of the healer's guard, "Everyone's dead, so I've brought her over for judgement. She must have done something to them." He dropped back into his normal voice and continued, "Or to put you with the rest of the townsfolk, since a true healer is too valuable to waste on revenge."

She gave him a wide-eyed stare. "That should rock them back on their heels a bit. How did you do that?" She looked frightened for the first time. "Is he in there with you?"

"What? No. *No!* I don't do *that*!" Zero shuddered. "Even if I'd killed him with my blade, I don't steal souls. I've just always been good at imitating voices."

"All right then. I'm sorry I reacted like that."

"You're handling everything happening today, including talking with me, a lot better than most of the people I deal with would," Zero said. Changing the subject, he asked, "Do you know where they are keeping the rest of the villagers in the building?"

"On the floor in the main room, tied up where they can easily watch them. They should still be there unless they've moved them. Occasionally, they'll take one of the women or older girls upstairs."

Zero growled softly, but it had been something he'd expected, even though the mixed gender units the humans had been forced to adopt due to the Great Black Death and the Mankiller and Rising Plagues had tempered military atrocities on civilians to a degree. Still, he wanted to stay as clear headed as possible, so he pulled out the pot of green salve and took a deep sniff of it. He felt more centered when he opened his eyes again. He was able to ask, without his temper flaring, "Are there more like Timothy among them?"

"None quite so bad as that, at least from how they've treated us. And no more weapons like the dirk you described among the ones still here."

That was a relief to learn. Zero hadn't quite been aware he'd dreaded facing another blade like the one Timothy had wielded. 'Among the ones still here' was a worry he'd deal with if or when the other raiders returned.

"Onward, then, I guess." She settled a heavy shawl across her shoulders against the chill of the sea fog and turned to Zero. "Better we surprise them."

Zero nodded. "I'll make my announcement and push you out of the way. Get yourself behind whatever cover you can. Start cutting loose whoever you know can fight. I'll keep the raiders distracted."

"May St. Michael and the Morrigan be with us," said Healer Greneglais.

They stepped out, Zero pretending to hurry her along for the benefit of anyone they might meet on the street.

The Drunken Fish, or the Salmon as the healer had named it, was quiet. Nothing seemed to have changed, except for the fog having thinned to a hazy veil and the shadow of the crag having angled further across the village.

Zero shoved open the door and pushed into the room. Townsfolk lay trussed along the walls and taking up most of the floor to the small bar. A hall next to it led back to a rear door and he could see part of the kitchen through an open arch. Stairs curled around themselves across the hall from the bar and an extension of the common room lay to his right with a fireplace on the same wall as the stairs.

Five raiders-by-their-garb and the fact they weren't tied like the rest were there. One sat behind the bar, the others eating hurriedly at a table near the fireplace.

"Get in, you," Zero said imitating the dead guard's voice, but modifying their plan for speed, and gave the healer a push. She stumbled forward a few steps and dropped down between two large villagers, the best cover available as the raiders had moved most of the other tables and chairs into the extension.

"You're here early," said the man behind the bar. "What's going -?" but before he could finish Zero had taken three quick steps across the room and put his handaxe into the man's head. That one fell backward off the stool he'd been sitting on, clutching his face.

Zero spun about, whirling his borrowed cloak off and by good luck deflecting a bolt from the quickest reacting of the men at the table. Sword out now and filling the room with its glow and angry hum, Zero lunged and whipped the blade's tip across the face of a man turning to toward him, dropping that one at least momentarily. He kicked the table, knocking it into the man with the crossbow. But the other two had made it to their feet and now the fight truly began.

They had long knives and barely longer swords, better suited for close work than the necroknight's sword. But a glowing, humming long blade wielded by someone of elven descent, someone who'd had more years of practice than the two of them combined, even before he'd died and Risen was more than a bit intimidating, even in cramped quarters. And with his borrowed cloak and hat shaken off, there was no way they could lie to themselves about what they were facing.

Zero pressed them, distracting one with the cloak spun to entangle blades while thrusting and slashing at the other. He managed to drop one of them with a blow to the temple, but by then the man he'd blocked with the overthrown table had regained his feet.

In general, humans were stronger, but elves faster. Being a necroknight, Zero had speed *and* unnatural strength, but this new pair of raiders were apparently used to fighting together and covered well for one another. The one he'd hit with the table had a basket-hilted long blade and kept trying to get through a blow to Zero's legs. The other tried to block and either bind up Zero's sword or get a strike on his sword arm.

Then in some unspoken agreement, the sword man launched a flurry of blows, while his partner stepped back and tried to circle around Zero's offhand.

Zero flipped the cape into the dagger-wielder's path, partially entangled his legs, and yanked the end of the cape back hard. The man tripped, stumbled, tried to recover, dropped one dagger, and fell over a villager, landing face first on the floor.

His partner got in a hard but glancing blow which scraped down Zero's arm and ripped the heavy cloth of the cloak out of his hand. Bits of leather, chainmail, and flesh went with the cloth, leaving Zero's arm tingling and only partly responsive, but he'd kept his opponent from being able to turn his painful but clumsy strike into yet another attempt at Zero's legs.

Basket-hilt brought his blade back on guard.

Zero pivoted and used his own like a dueling sabre, forcing the man back with rapid jabs and strikes into the knocked-over table where he, like his partner, also tripped and fell.

The man scrambled desperately to get up, only to find Zero's sword in the hollow of his throat.

"Lie still and live a bit longer," Zero cautioned him, but he tried to jerk away and Zero was at the end of whatever patience he had left and thrust forward with his blade.

"You chose stupidly," the necroknight told the twitching body, whipping his blade back out and whirling to see what might yet be about to attack.

Several solid women were just rising from the area behind the bar. Other villagers, still tied, were watching Zero with wide, worried eyes, while several of their freed companions had swarmed over the remaining stunned or injured raiders. The struggle there was bloody, but brief as the villagers took revenge on their captors.

Then Healer Greneglais pushed through them and hurried to his side.

"Let me see your arm," she demanded.

"What?"

"Your arm, man! You're cut to the bone!"

Zero looked at it. "Well," he said, still not feeling the wound. "There's another shirt ruined. And the bastard cut right through my vambrace."

"Sit," ordered the healer. It seemed like a reasonable idea, so Zero sat, while she peeled back layers and did something with his arm involving a sewing needle and heavy thread. And the use of the pot of green ointment, which mostly countered the scents of blood and dying and calmed Zero's bloodlust.

"Aren't there people I still need to go kill?" Zero asked, trying not to watch the woman sewing his arm back together and not fidget under her touch.

"It be quite entirely possible we can handle at least soom o' that, laddie," said one of the old villagers now standing guard in the tavern. "Ye took doon five men by yersel'. I'd say ye earned a si'doon fer a wee spell."

Zero nodded. He didn't really need it, but it was nice, if a bit confusing to have someone fussing over him and mending his wound. And the villagers would feel better if they got to get some of their own back, without an outsider 'rescuing' them. Provided they could do it without too many of them getting injured or killed.

***

The dead had been dragged out, the bloodied sawdust shoveled up and thrown into the fire, and food set to cooking before the parents returned with their children. Triumphant and grateful, but they were turning to worry again as Zero warned of the illness affecting their neighbors south along the High Road.

"I promised I would be back to the MacLeans tonight," he told them, thinking it seemed the same as every battle he'd been in - a lifetime passed in a bottle only to be uncorked to flow once again with the rest of the world. It was still not quite dark on the same day as he'd set out from the MacLeans' farm.

He took up the reins of the ever-hungry, but unflappable chestnut horse he'd commandeered for himself. "Ten rode out, Light only knows when they'll be back. Or if. And only you might guess if there are others out roving as well. But I'll be back. With whoever I can gather to help."

He hoped it would be by mid-morning, with Geoffrey, the MacLean children, and the MacIver clan, as he continued, "The Great House seems full of crossbows, send a party up there to recover them and as many bolts as you can find. Burn the dead. Hold the tavern. And retreat into the tunnels or the sea, if you must."

He swung his leg easily over the gelding's back - easily because he was standing on the wall outside the Drunken Fish - and settled into the saddle. "If I'm not back, it'll be because of raiders at the MacLeans or the MacIvers. My warmount will soon be coming back through from Thornhill, likely with at least one Caliburn Knight following her. Watch for them."

"Godspeed, Zerollen diGriz," Healer Greneglais told him.

Zero clucked to the placid gelding and twitched the reins. It flicked one ear back at him and started off at a walk.

"As best my mount will grant," he joked, and tapped it lightly with his heel.

6: WHAT MOVES IN THE NIGHT AND IN THE DAY

The cob broke into a trot which was easy to post, and the short distance to the damaged bridge and the path beside the Craigburn was quickly covered. The water was down off the deck of the bridge, but not so much he was willing to try the crossing. If he'd had Bessariel with him, he wouldn't have hesitated, but with the lazy cob, he was much less inclined to take risks. A trot along the stream though the low fog still curling up from the soggy ground was safer, if an annoying detour.

He couldn't probe ahead as he would have been able to do while riding his warmount for fear of panicking the slow chestnut, but there wasn't any place along the path thick enough to set an ambush. He let the cob gelding drop back to a walk where there were turns tight enough to block his view.

Just as on his trip north, the path remained empty of threats and the thinned fog let him see the other bank as well, until it finally got too dark to make out details across the Craigburn. By then he was across the old military bridge and started down the other side. He switched to leading the horse through the narrow footpath and rocky areas, but even walking, they made much better time than he had limping along that morning.

He reached the MacIvers' holding in time for the late evening milking, passing out the medicine Healer Greneglais had sent while sharing the story of what transpired in Invercraig. Molly MacIver mixed up the powder for the MacLean children while her daughters dosed their own household. As soon as the draughts were ready and wrapped for travel, Zero was back in the saddle and switching the reluctant cob into a canter for the dash to the MacLean farm – at least where the road allowed for it.

Geoffrey and Bannock greeted him in the farmyard where Zero left the sweating horse to be cooled out by Geoff while he ran inside to dose the children. Once he'd spooned the last drops into Mary-wee and Hector had finished dosing his older sister, they gathered in the barn to give the cob a rub down and share news.

"They did *what*?" Geoff snarled, sweeping a twist of straw over the cob's shaggy winter coat and stripping off long swaths of loose hair.

Zero gave him the short version, working on the gelding's other side with a wooden comb and likewise removing heavy clumps of hair.

"Great God in Heaven! What possessed Dyer to take the town like that? That wasn't the way he operated."

He peered over the gelding's back at Zero. "We weren't saints by any reach, but putting Timothy as a guard on children? Timothy was the reason no women would ride with us. We'd have been better off if we'd put that bastard on the gibbet ourselves."

"Why didn't you?

"As far as I could tell?" Geoff replied. "He could fire a bolt through a keyhole and hit his target nine times out of ten. And he was worth three men in combat, especially against the Risen. But there were times Dyer had him chained to a barn post as well. They'd rode together for a long time, since they'd been in the Polish kingdoms at least. That might have been it."

Geoff picked up the cob's front hoof and started picking dirt out. "But things had been getting odd the further north we came. After we left Invar Nis and the sickness started hitting? That's when we started 'requisitioning' mounts and food from the villages and holts. Even then, we were leaving some token payment."

He put the hoof down and went to the cob's hind leg. "I don't remember much about arriving here. I was already out of it with fever. But from what you told me, they just left me wander off and didn't even come looking for me. I mean, what good Christian would leave a man to drown and then just let the body there in the water?"

Zero gave Geoffrey a side-eye he couldn't see with the horse between them and said, "Geoff, you don't want to know the things I've seen 'good Christians' do. But deliberately fouling the water in friendly territory? That's -," he cast about for a description, since Hector was milking the cow nearby. "That's not done."

The old warmount wandered in from the pasture and leaned against the gate. When that didn't get him a response, he whickered and stamped a foot.

"What's with you, old man?" asked Hector.

The warmount carefully mouthed the gate and rattled it.

Zero looked over his shoulder at the beast, who flicked an ear at him, and then rattled the gate again.

"Hungry?" asked Hector, but the skinny old warmount distinctly shook his head and stamped a hoof again.

"I don't think so," said Zero. "Let him out, Hector."

"You're sure?"

"Better than having him going through or over your gate." Zero patted the cob gelding. "Geoff, you done with that foot?"

"Good here," said the necroknight squire, stepping away from the cob.

Zero led the horse into one of the stalls as Hector let the bigger mount into the runway. It confidently took the place the cob had previously occupied, apparently waiting to be groomed in turn. "That's what I thought," said Zero. "Has he said –"

Hector looked from the warmount to Zero to Geoffrey and back to the warmount, his eyes going huge. "He said to get ready, that something's coming."

"Well, that clears up who he's picked as a rider," said Zero, latching the cob in for the moment. He handed Hector the comb. "You groom him, I'll get your sisters ready to move – we'll be easier able to defend against raiders if we get to the MacIvers. Geoffrey, get the tack back on the cob and throw down more fodder for the cows."

Geoff turned to get the chestnut's bridle and saddle, muttering about taking orders from a horse and overreacting.

Ignoring Geoffrey's complaint, Zero turned back to Hector and the warmount, asking, "Did the raiders leave any tack for him?"

"No," said Hector, already running the comb through the big mount's coat. "But I cleaned up our old bridle, I've just never tried it on him. The only reins we have are for plowing or driving though."

"I'm not worried so much about you needing a bridle as not sliding off him if he moves suddenly. That's where a saddle is useful."

Shaking his head, Zero started for the house. "I'll come up with something. Make sure his shoes aren't loose."

The girls seemed about the same as when Zero and Hector had given them the medicine. He pulled heavier clothing out for them from their shared wardrobe and proceeded to layer the clothing on them until he thought he might be able to prop them upright and not have them fall over. A growing prickle of alarm kept him moving, back out to the barn where he found both horse and warmount ready and Bannock having brought in the cow and her calf in from the paddock.

"Hector?"

The boy, with Geoffrey's aid, had harnessed the warmount and hitched him to a small cart. Hector was now perched on the mount's back. "Yes, sir?"

"If you know where any treasures your family had-"

"I was thinking that too, Sir Zero," he said gravely. "I'll be right back."

He slid down, patted his mount, and ran for the house. "His name is Broken Sky," he yelled back over his shoulder.

Geoffrey came over to the cart with an armload of hay. "Are the two of them just making me antsy or is something actually going on?"

Broken Sky flicked an ear back and snorted.

"I'm pretty certain something's coming," said Zero. "Once you have a warmount of your own, you'll understand. They hear and see things we don't or can't without really working at it. So, trust your mount when you find them. Horses were already made to look for predators; when the first ones became warmounts it seems like their senses expanded fivefold, at least."

"Think we should go to the trouble to take the cows?" Geoff asked. "The horse – Broken Sky, sorry, and Bannock seemed to have some conversation going while you were inside and then the dog ran out and brought the cows into the barn."

"I think that's a sure sign of something bad coming. Let's leave as little here for whatever it is to find as we can."

"Thought so." Geoffrey picked up a pair of long wicker crates and set them in the cart, provoking a few sleepy complaints from the hens he'd stuffed inside.

The old warmount, as though he'd been waiting just for the chickens to be loaded, leaned into the collar and started across the yard to the house. Zero let the cow and her calf out, Bannock nipping at her heels to move the cow along. Zero took the long-handled scythe as well, balancing it on his shoulder as they went.

Geoffrey got the chestnut cob and his bow and quiver of hunting arrows. They might not be as deadly against an armored foe as war arrows, but depending on placement, could still do a good bit of harm.

Broken Sky parked the cart close enough to the doorway, Zero and Geoff could barely squeeze inside, but the closeness made it convenient when they loaded the girls and wrapped them well with all the dry blankets and extra clothing they had hanging in the entry.

Hector came struggling down from somewhere upstairs, holding a cask almost as big as himself and carrying a wheat dolly between his teeth. With Geoffrey's help, he got both into the cart by the girls' feet, before getting a leg up onto Broken Sky's back.

The old warmount stood until the boy was firmly settled, then threw himself into a trot, jerking the cart into swift motion. Bannock set the cow forward, her calf trotting around her in confusion. Geoff slid onto the cob's back with Zero's help. Zero recovered the scythe and started trotting after the cows. Geoffrey managed to flick the reluctant cob into motion and soon caught up with him.

Thunder rumbled somewhere in the mountains and a cold wind rushed down from the heights heavy with the scent of freshly turned earth. Zero and Geoffrey exchanged glances. The ground was barely warm enough and too wet for anyone to have been plowing in the mountains. Broken Sky shifted to pacing and the cart fairly flew forward. The chestnut cob gave a little squeal and surprised Zero - and Geoffrey, no doubt - by actually sprinting after the warmount, leaving him and Bannock to bring up the unconcerned cow and calf.

The road wasn't in good enough repair for Broken Sky to keep up his pace for long, but Zero was still losing ground on the cart at every smooth section of the road until another scent blew down from the highlands. Stomach-turning corruption rode on the wind, heavy enough Zero expected the contents of some nearby battlefield or graveyard had suddenly been turned out. He gave the cow up for lost and ran for the MacIvers and Bannock ran with him. But the cow, perhaps old enough to have run from Risen as a calf, recognized the smell of death and broke into a gallop herself, urging her calf forward until all of them turned off the road into the relatively safety of the MacIvers' steading.

***

Old Alasdair MacIver brought a jug of his family's whisky and a teapot out to the stable where Zero and Geoffrey were keeping watch with Hector and Broken Sky. Currently, the boy was sleeping atop his mount, one of his family's blankets covering them both.

A pair of Alasdair's granddaughters passed by, walking the immediate bounds of the steading with salted water and smoking incense. A husband or brother, Zero wasn't certain which from the hurried round of introductions paced them with a bow, ready to draw and let fly arrows. All three also carried maces. One of them was also reciting from a prayer book, either of the Scottish Kirk or of something older as well.

As they passed, certain stones set in the wall glowed a faint blue.

"I miss the old place down on the Border," said Alasdair. "But this is a good stead and stronger than the one we lost. My son chose well when he married into the Highlands. And Molly's been a strong chieftain and a good mother. And a good daughter to me, as dear as if she were mine and Maggie's own. Still, it's good to have an old friend to stand with when things as shouldn't be walking the land come 'round."

He poured another wee dram for himself and Zero and one for Geoffrey too. "Good to have new friends as well, young Hartsbane."

Not long after Alasdair had again sought out his bed, in the darkest, coldest hour of the night, Broken Sky stood with all his attention focused to the south. Hector stirred in his sleep and said clearly, "They come."

Zero spread the warning to the nearest MacIvers on watch just before the barrier their sisters had reinforced lit with a steady blue glow. It flared here and there as the enemy tested it. But they were only along the road.

For all the stomach-emptying stench of slaughter on the wind, a mere handful of Risen, and those only skeletons, had appeared. The MacIvers' arcane wards held them off easily.

"Stay with Hector and Broken Sky," Zero told Geoffrey and raced a quick circle on foot around the inside of the farmstead's wall, checking briefly with those standing watch at key points and probing the darkness beyond until he was back with his companions again.

"Nothing," he told them. "Whatever is causing this is following the road."

"Could they be hiding from you?" Geoffrey asked.

"If they had enough power to hide from me *and* Broken Sky both, they wouldn't be slowed by those wards. Someone's sending out a big fear effect; I'd guess to see what stands their ground and what might come out looking." He watched the skeletons spread out along the road, reminding him of an honor guard before something wafted into view. For all that it was trying to pass itself off as a bodiless undead, with cobwebby illusions and horrible smells, Zero could tell it was human. And mortal. But no less dangerous for that.

"Come out. Return to the service of your true ruler," it called. It was trying hard, but even a normal mortal having once seen a true ghost and survived wasn't likely to be fooled by its act. But there was power behind the command.

Geoffrey took an involuntary step forward.

"Steady," said Zero. "You are not its to call."

Geoffrey shuddered all over and stepped back. "How did he *do* that?"

"*It*," said Zero, giving the being no respect, "is a resurrectionist. What you Anglish call a necromancer. They have power similar to ours. And you weren't prepared for the pull."

"Could it control me?"

"Not with me here," said Zero with certainty. "Even if the wards fail. And now you know what one feels like, so even if you don't consciously know one's around, your spirit will recognize that pull and deny it."

"I can feel you in there," came the voice again. "You cannot resist me. Come forth!"

"Ah!" Geoffrey winced, but held his place. "I see what you mean."

"See if you can hit it from here," Zero suggested.

Geoffrey notched an arrow and let fly into the thickest patch of swirling whiteness.

The illusions dissipated and a scrawny human of indeterminate age and sex in a black cassock crumpled to the road.

The MacIvers cheered.

"That seemed too easy," said Geoffrey.

Zero nodded.

Broken Sky snapped his tail from side to side and stomped a hoof, striking sparks from his metal shoe. His opinion was clear enough, even to someone unused to being around a warmount.

The wards' glow increased until everything was faintly lit with blue.

The skeletons still stood there, waiting.

A black garbed rider on something like a black horse resolved out of the darkness.

It looked down at the crumpled figure.

It gestured and the figure rose to its hands and feet and scuttled after its master, joining three others who followed the rider like hounds.

The rider turned its head to look directly at Zero, Geoffrey, Broken Sky, and Hector, awake again just in time to see it pass. Red sparks suggested eyes under a dark hat brim. It inclined its head slightly.

Then it rode on, ghouls following, and the skeletons joining the group as the rider passed them on the road.

***

Dawn was vivid after the days of drizzle and fog, everything sparkling with a washed-clean freshness. The sunlight seemed particularly bright and warm after the slow hours spent in watching once the necromancer and its pack of undead had passed. They had not returned. A quick gallop along the outer bounds of the farm held only fading traces of their passing and those only along the Craigburn.

By the time Zero, Geoffrey, and the MacIver riders returned to the steading, those who had remained behind could report some of the less sick were already starting to feel better. But two of the MacIver's youngest, along with Aggie and Mary-wee, didn't seem to be responding to the medicine yet.

"We may need to see if we can get them to Healer Greneglais," Molly MacIver suggested. "She's got all of her remedies and supplies to make others there in Invercraig, rather than bringing her out here where I might not have what she'd need in my stocks. Girls, you'll need to ride out to the bridge and see what needs done to repair it or rig a way across the burn."

After a short argument on which method would be wiser, they decided to take tools with them, so they wouldn't have to be running back and forth. Two of the women began gathering ropes and timbers and planks from a storage barn, while others hitched horses for spreading manure on the field and plowing the driest of them. Another one was harnessed for pulling their wagon of repair supplies to the bridge. Old Alasdair climbed up to the bell tower to relieve the boy on watch. By the time hammers and spikes had been added to the wagon and oatmeal cakes and water jugs stored away for the midday meal, the plowwoman was already turning over the first furrows in the best drained of their fields behind her sister and brother pitching manure from the cart ahead of her. A pair of the healthy younger girls were on watch along the far edges of the close field, also gathering storm-downed branches for their stubby isle ponies to drag back to the house.

"If you hear the bell or sight that witchy-thing or anything else coming, drop what you're doing and make for the stead."

"Aye, Mum. We'll be careful."

Her eldest daughter gave Molly a hug and a peck and then climbed up to the driving box and clucked to the horse. The gelding gave himself a shake, then leaned into his collar and set off at a slow jog, several of the other MacIvers trotting along on foot or riding in the back of the wagon.

"Where do you want us?" Zero asked.

"Riding scout or, if you would, giving a hand to my girls with some of the heavier timbers, if they're needed for the bridge. I'd rather have you out to give us warning if that foul witch-thing or those raiders come back."

Zero nodded and turned to tighten the girth on the lazy chestnut. Geoffrey gave the woman a wave which might have been half a salute and turned his borrowed horse out to the road. Zero joined him there after getting a boost up onto the chestnut.

"Guard or scout?" Geoffrey asked as they followed the MacIver women along the road.

Zero tugged the chestnut's head back up and tapped him into a trot. "I'd like to keep you with me, but I'm thinking of ranging out to the military road. You'd be better here in case anything comes up out of the burn to trouble the workers."

When they got to the bridge, some of the folks from Invercraig were already examining the span from their side of the stream. The oldest MacIver daughter got into a yelling across the burn conversation with what seemed to be the town's blacksmith, while some of the others climbed down to take a closer look at the base of the pillars. Worry was expressed about whether the flooding had scoured the streambed under the piers and whether one of the beams was cracked.

Zero left Geoffrey to keep watch while the engineering details were figured out and urged the chestnut along the footpath slowly. He alternated scanning the bush, flush with early spring color, but no leaves yet burst from their buds, with looking for signs of the necromancer's passing. Especially here along the recently flooded burn, the scents of fresh mud and warming earth were strong and the grass seemed greener in the sunlight. He also snapped a low-hanging branch stretching toward the burn at face-height and showed it to the chestnut. "Mind, you great empty belly," he warned. "You haven't been turned out for grazing."

The chestnut laid back his ears and tried to ram his head down to the ground again, but Zero was having none of that. And when the horse leaped and began a series of bucks, he held fast as a burr until the chestnut finally settled again.

"Guess it's good to see having a warmount hasn't ruined me for riding you silly beasts. Onward, you lazy lob."

Apparently agreeable to continuing now it had determined Zero knew what he was doing, the chestnut actually moved out at a good ground-covering walk along the footpath. Zero was able to go back to keeping a watch for bad footing and ambushes. The further he got from the coastal road, the clearer it became the path was seldom used by riders. Branches he'd not really noticed during his ride back the previous night hung down or reached out from the side of the path opposite the Craigburn. They were too high to bother someone walking or running, but once he was beyond the

MacIvers' farm, they became more and more of a nuisance to him as a rider.

Signs the necromancer had found them annoying as well became more and more common the further he rode. Small branches were also more and more often snapped off, occasionally with the offending tip still dangling by a strip of bark. Or they were found bent over, their woody stem cracked, but not broken off completely. And in soft spots, the ground was finally showing hoofprints and the tracks of the ghouls overlaying his own earlier tracks.

At one point, the dark rider must have finally reached the end of their patience with a particular overgrown thorny sloe and blighted the shrub, which was still withering and dying back when Zero noticed it. It seemed odd, since the blackthorn sloe was considered a tree of the darker side of magicks, but the necromancer's ire might have further been provoked by the rowan growing behind it.

On a whim, Zero stopped, tethered the chestnut, and used his own minor necromantic power to back-burn the blight out of what remained of the sloe bush.

"Oh, well done!" said a pair of voices behind him. Turning in wary haste, he saw two maidens dressed in white, one with red hair and the other with black, standing by the chestnut who was nosing them curiously. The black-haired maiden was disfigured all along her right side.

Zero's eyes widened in surprise. Then he dropped his gaze slightly and bowed deeply in the elven fashion to them both.

"Ladies of the Trees," he said.

"Nay," said the black-tressed maiden. "Do not bow to me, Sir Knight of the Shadows-Between. I owe thee mine own life for thine mercy, painful as it might have been. How may I aid thee?"

Even for one of the deenee shee, bargaining with the truly spirit folk could be dangerous. But after a stunned moment blinking, Zero thought quickly of aid the blackthorn maiden would be willing to provide. "I ride in service to others, but as soon as I am free of my promises, I ride in hunt of the dark one. Would you let me seek the one who harmed you with an item of your favour to hand?"

A wicked, needle-toothed smile spread across the tree fay's face. "Oh, most surely I will, Sir. Take up some of my winter fallen branches and I will make for thee a favour most puissant."

Zero gathered several thorny branches from the ground on the undamaged side of the blackthorn and carefully handed them to the maiden.

Moving with the careful hesitation of one still wounded, she stripped a handful of thorns from the limbs. Drawing them out in length and binding several together with strands of her long black hair, she spoke a charm over them, which she repeated until nine slender needle-headed arrows fletched with feathers of the birds which loved blackthorn best were gathered in her hand. These she wrapped in a sleeve taken from her dress and presented to Zero, along with a twisted, spiked and knobbed club-like rod she crafted of the remaining branches. She completed the arming with a sprig of profusely flowering blackthorn which she bound into the band of his hat.

The rowan maiden also offered him a gift, an equal-armed sunwheel of rowan twigs bound with red thread. "For as my sister protected me, so will this be a shield against the one you seek."

"Share the arrows with the one you call Hartsbane," suggested the blackthorn maiden.

Zero bowed low again. He wondered how the tree maid knew about Geoffrey, but trees and spirits talked to each other.

This time when he rose, the maidens had gone, but sprigs of blackthorn and rowan blooming out of season adorned the chestnut's bridle, mane, and tail.

He tied the bundle of arrows carefully to the saddle. After checking the girth again, he also took a moment to pick out the chestnut's hooves before swinging astride.

The chestnut carried him quickly and without further incident to the military road, where he ascertained the necromancer's trail continued down that smoother road and made no turn off onto the wide path leading back to Invercraig.

Returning downstream again, he saw what remained of the thorny black sloe bush was now a defiant mass of white blossoms as he passed by. He nodded to the tree maidens, though he didn't see them. Politeness was always appreciated. In some cases, expected by the fae.

The muddy, rocky path still made for a slow ride. But the ride itself was uneventful, if you didn't count the number of blackthorn sloe which were now pushing out their first blossom buds.

The MacIvers and the townsfolk had cleared the broken bridge decking and put some sort of patch along one of the beams in the time he'd been gone. Now they were resurfacing the deck of the bridge with new planks.

Geoffrey stepped out of his guard spot and waved Zero over, looking curiously at the flowers adorning the chestnut gelding and his tack, and the crown of Zero's hat. "What?" he asked, gesturing at the flowers.

"I found something the dark rider had done and countered it to spite them. Some of my mother's distant relatives approved."

Geoffrey opened his mouth, thought better of whatever he'd been about to say, and shut it again. He did much the same when Zero handed him eight of the special arrows and his handaxe.

"It looks like they've been busy," Zero continued. "Any problems?"

"They needed me to help with holding the beam in place until they got enough spikes or screws in. Otherwise, it has been boring, unless you're interested in how bridges are put together. There was a lot of talk about getting down to the pillars and checking the streambed for scouring, whatever that is, but the water is still too high for them to do it."

"Scouring's when the water comes so fast it digs the ground right out from under the support," said a woman who was eating her midday meal nearby. "That's why you'll see good stone cladding on the upstream side of bridge pillars to split the force of the water and keep it from undermining them. That's why the old Roman bridges are still there when new ones wash out." She went on at some length about bridge design and how she'd like to see a new stone bridge put up, "Though that's as likely as having the roads repaired. No one's got the money to pay for the quarrying or smoothing the stones, much less hauling them here."

Zero could have told her road repair was being done, but it was still likely to be a year or more before the stone mages and other workers made it to Invercraig. It certainly didn't help at the moment.

They continued to keep watch. Geoffrey left to scout down to the shore and along the coast for a short distance, but found nothing which seemed threatening.

By late afternoon, the bridge was almost completed, and the wagon was sent back to gather the sick children.

The woman who'd talked to them about bridge building had a fine sense of timing and the last plank was fitted into the decking just before the wagon returned. Hector and Broken Sky came along with the wagon and the warmount was the first horse to cross the repaired span.

Once Broken Sky had stomped around on the bridge to his satisfaction, the wagon with the sick children crossed with Hector and Bannock trotting alongside and Zero following on the chestnut gelding. Geoffrey returned his borrowed horse to the MacIvers and came after on foot.

Leaving the wagon horse and the chestnut tethered, everyone crowded into Goody Greneglais's house, which now smelled of fresh meadowsweet and lavender. Geoffrey stopped at the threshold with a yelp and had to be invited in specifically by the healer, after she studied him for a long moment. Once he was inside, she surprised him by taking his hand and pulling him into the room where the children were being put bed.

"Tell me what you see," she commanded firmly.

"What I see?" The Anglish necroknight looked around in confusion.

"The shadow you told us you saw over them?" Zero prompted.

"Oh! That!" Geoffrey took a deep breath and sighed it out, letting his eyes go unfocused. After a moment in which the arcane glow across them seemed to brighten, he began describing what he'd previously mentioned as 'a sort of cloud around them.'

Healer Greneglais frowned and rubbed between her eyes, then disappeared into another room, coming back with a book she was leafing carefully through. Taking a seat near the hearth where the lighting was brightest, she began asking detailed questions on the color, shape, and density of the clouds he saw around the children. The MacIver women listened with interest while Zerollen and Hector exchanged glances both confused and worried.

After this had gone on for a while, Goody Greneglais looked over at Zero and asked, "Can I keep him?"

"Ah, he's not mine to give," Zero replied, somewhat flustered. He looked at Geoffrey, who seemed equally surprised.

"I supposed you could lend me to her," Geoffrey said slowly. "But I'm fairly certain I've not had enough training to stay for any length of time around," he cast about for the words. "Around normal people," he finally settled on. "And you're the only one I know who might be able to teach me."

"Well, then," said Zero. "I suppose you'll do the most good here. Make sure you stay warm and keep fed. Getting hungry is the worst thing you could do right now."

"That being said, milady," Geoff inclined his head to the healer, "I'm yours for the duration."

"I understand," she said. "Of course, you'll be free to leave. But you'd be a very great help to me in treating the children right now, if you could stay with me until we can break this illness."

She shot a firm look at the oldest MacIver in the room. "Go tell Molly to send in anyone else who isn't rallying from medicines I sent. Tell her this has gone beyond a normal sickness. Hector MacLean, if you could stay to lend a general hand and run errands for me? That would also be a great help."

"I'd like to, milady, but—" Hector fidgeted nervously, ducking his head and twisting a foot in the rushes and meadowsweet on the floor. "But I've got a warmount and he'd not had the best care before he came to me. I have to see to his comfort first."

"Well, of course you do," Healer Greneglais said. "If that's all that's worrying you about staying, you can put him in the garden, if he needs to be close. I've a little shed where he can get out of the weather back there. Just ask him to respect the herb beds and not eat the chickens."

She looked to Zero and Geoffrey, "I'm sorry. I'd completely forgotten about warmounts. Do you need to keep yours here as well?"

"I don't have one yet," said Geoffrey.

"And mine isn't back from Thornhill," added Zero.

"Thornhill? You had mentioned that. Quite a distance for an unaccompanied horse. How'd – Nevermind, I'll find out later if I need to. Now I need to examine these children. Lydia, why don't you take your sisters home and check on things there and I'll be expecting someone back this evening. Hector and Sir -?" she looked around.

"Hartsbane, milady. Geoffrey Hartsbane."

"Why don't you come with me, Sir Hartsbane, and I'll show you both the kitchen and where to find things. Sir diGriz? Are you staying?"

"I'll be back, but I'm going to escort the ladies to the bridge first."

"Safe travels then. And I'll see you back here shortly."

***

Zero was able to escort the MacIvers to the bridge without incident. He was even able to get Lazy Lob up to a canter for part of the way back. He stopped where he'd killed the chestnut's original rider to make sure no one had missed finding the body, but it wasn't there. Hoping it had been removed by someone from the village and not wandered off on its own - despite his having taken precautions to prevent it - he trotted back to Invercraig and went looking for someone who could tell him whether it had been found or not.

The Drunken Fish seemed to be one of the centers for the village, so he stopped there first and was fortunate enough to find the very person who'd recovered the body and taken it to the pyre site on the beach. Leaving the tavern, he took the chestnut down to the hiring stable near the mill.

The gelding recognized where they were going and actually picked up the pace, lifting his head and sniffing loudly. He whickered in excitement on catching the scent of other horses and Zero felt him tense to bolt, checking him into a tight circling.

"Were you gelded late, old man?" Zero asked while they circled. "What did I tell you about trying to pull tricks with me?"

Lob settled, perhaps dizzy from the circling, and walked politely the rest of the way to the stable.

There were a surprisingly large number of horses there, most out in a dry paddock where they crowded the rails to investigate the new arrival. Their whinnies brought out the stable master and her daughter to take Lob in for a good rub down and hoof picking, before Zero saw him put into one of the empty stalls and given a small measure of oats and several forkfuls of hay. A large bucket of clean water from the stable's catchment finished bedding the gelding in for the night. Zero carefully took the still fresh sprigs of blackthorn sloe and rowan from the bridle and stuck them through his hatband next to the flowers already braided there. He left the ones braided into the gelding's mane and tail where they were.

He came out on the street to find Geoffrey pacing down toward the mill, counting his steps out loud as he walked.

"What're you up to?"

"Pacing out distances for my bow, for when Dyer comes back," the Anglish necroknight said grimly. "And Goody Greneglais sent me down to the pyre with some special oil for the burning tonight."

They walked down to the shore together to where all of the raider dead had been carried. The number of them was sobering. They were laid out on a pile of driftwood with peat stacked around them. Zero handed Geoffrey some of the blackthorn and rowan he'd taken from Lazy Lob's adornments, much to the squire's bemusement.

"Good men and bad," said Geoffrey looking at the dead after he'd woven the plant stems into the cloak pin holding the blanket he'd claimed for a weather cape. "And it seems like the sickness took most of the good ones. I wonder what that says about me?"

He stood turning the pot of oil the herbwife had given him around in his hands for a long moment. "May we get what we deserve, in God's Name." Geoffrey cracked the seal over the lid and began carefully pouring a bit of oil on the head of each body. He seemed to be reciting a prayer for the dead under his breath while he did so.

Zero stepped back, turning to catch the offshore wind swooping down from the North Sea. He hated burnings, but there wasn't anything more certain for keeping possibly tainted bodies from rising than to give them to the flames. And it wasn't even the flames which bothered him as much as the smell, though some necroknights were inclined to panic when faced with fire. Few undead of any type were comfortable with flames, even if they had been pyromancers in life.

He wanted to get Geoffrey and himself away before the vicar came, but it seemed Goodwoman Greneglais had given his squire a job to do. Thankfully, the Anglish former raider had finished and was able to pass the now-emptied oil pot off to the pale young vicar who came down to the beach at dusk, along with a number of the townsfolk.

Geoffrey seemed as anxious to leave the pyre behind as Zero, his steps long and quick, forcing his shorter companion to hurry to keep up. Once they were back to the main road, he started pacing and counting his way again toward the northern gate. "I've got bodkin heads," he said, naming the arrows designed specifically for punching through armor. "But not many. More bolts for the crossbows. No pistols, Dyer took every one of them he could find."

"Think there are any here he couldn't find?"

"Possibly." Geoffrey looked down at Zero. "You should probably be the one asking. No one seems to recognize me, though of course, this is my first time here. But you're closer to being accepted by them than I'm likely to be. Especially after rescuing their children."

"I see you've been hearing stories."

"Mainly from the herbwitch. She thinks well of you." Geoffrey paused in his measuring of the town and stretched. "Is she fey? She seems to know a lot about necroknights and elves and such."

"Healers know about us because they've had to deal with the harm we can cause. You're a knight of the

Yellow Horse or so it seems, aware of the fluctuations of the living. I'm more aligned with the White, winter and necromancy. And all necroknights serve the Red Horse of War," said Zero, "so healers are constantly at odds with us. But for milady healer specially? All I can say is her use name means green grey in Anglish. And green is a color of the Shee and the other Folk."

"I think I'm more confused now than I was before I asked. Did you just say you don't know? Or that you can't tell me?"

Zero chuckled. "Isn't that what my mother's people are said to do? Confuse humans?"

"And never give an hon—" Geoffrey bit off what he'd started to say and finished, "Yes."

"Then I say more clearly, no, I don't know. But green is also the color of life and growing things. Think on that for a bit."

Geoffrey snorted, but also shook his head. "I will. In the time I have between figuring out the best places to slow down Dyer when he comes back. Don't let them think the church would be a good refuge, he'd burn it around them, and loot what he could from the rubble. The same with the tavern. Is the keep defensible?"

"More than here. Even if we had a full wall, we don't have enough fighters to hold the town. If the old laird will let them in, the Great House will be easier to defend. And I think he will. He helped me with the children."

"A ghost?" Geoffrey asked doubtfully.

"The Laird's ghost. And these are still his people to defend."

"Well, maybe you can convince them of that. I need to finish walking the bounds. Meet you at the tavern?"

"Or the hospice. And remember to get yourself a warm drink."

"I've hot tea in a flask inside my gambeson."
"Good hunting, then. See you in a bit."

***

There were women in pairs or with an older child or the rare surviving man out now, all of them armed, all of them trying to be hidden. But the scent of burning meat was on the occasional draft of air from the coast and that alone was enough to bring scavengers, mortal or otherwise. Though Zero was walking openly through the darkening lanes, he was also scanning for what else might be moving or lurking in the shadows.

He'd taken the looping lane up and passed the graveyard and church and back down to the healer's home. She and Hector weren't there, but one of the women who was sitting with the children told him they'd gone for dinner at the Salmon. Zero started out the back to look in on the warmount. But the water in the kettle was still warm, so he first poured himself a drink and sat by the hearth until he'd finished it before going out to check on the old horse. Broken Sky was delicately cropping the sparse grass in the back yard and only flicked an ear at him. Leaving through the front gate, he went to join Hector and the herbwife at what he still thought of as the Drunken Fish.

The tavern was full of warmth and mostly good smells as many of the villagers not on guard duty or burning the dead raiders seemed to be taking their dinner there. "Ah, good. You're here," the old bartender greeted him. "Sir Knight, what do you think about us removing ourselves to the Laird's Great House? Could we defend it against the raiders?"

"Better than trying to hold the town," Zero said, shuffling to the side of the door to leave it clear while not crowding those eating close by. Between his own presence and the blackthorn flowers' unique scent fresh in the favour he wore, he knew some of the more sensitive humans present might be put off their meal.

"That's what we thought. We've been packing our goods all day to either go there or to Molly MacIver's steading," the old woman agreed.

"That would be another good choice, but you'd be like peas in a pod there. And Craig House would be harder for anyone to take."

"Ayeup, that's why we sent some up there to fix the doors this morning and clear paths to the well and stables." She turned, waving an encouraging hand to the room, "Eat up folks! We'll want to start moving there tonight." Looking to the healer, she asked, "Goody Greneglais, you'll need help moving the children, won't you?"

"I'd like to leave them at my place as long as I can –"

Hector jumped upright, eyes widening, breaking over the conversation, "Broken Sky says Geoffrey needs help, Sir Zerollen!"

Zero spun back for the door, saying, "Get folks moving. Now!" Hector started to follow, but the healer caught his arm before he could dart after the necroknight.

Then Zero was out onto the street, casting his awareness out like a fishing net seeking Geoffrey, while blinking the tavern light out of his eyes. He heard Broken Sky scream a warning like an angry stallion, joined by Bannock and perhaps half a dozen other dogs suddenly setting up a howl that swept the village.

Breaking into a run, he headed back toward the hospice and the southwest corner of Invercraig. He could feel Geoffrey now, feel his squire startle, then recognize his partner's presence. They knew where each other was now.

Zero could also feel - almost hear – other undead pushing closer. He wasn't certain how many were coming. Nor why he hadn't felt them when he'd been with the warmount only minutes before.

Nor where those undead were exactly, except for somewhere beyond the point Geoffrey was holding. Others. Similar to the necroknights, but not as powerful. Not even as powerful as Geoffrey. But coming closer. Risen. Most likely ghouls. And with increasing certainty he knew there were more than the four he'd seen last night.

He felt his lips curl into a feral, tooth-showing grin. And he drew his sword.

The weapon vibrated in his hand and just barely visible purple-black shadow swept down the blade like hoarfrost forming on metal.

He hurtled the woven fence of the hospice, landing in the herb garden, and went sprinting across the yard to the low stone wall along the Craigburn path. Broken Sky stood there, almost invisible, pale and dappled against the pale and shadow-dappled stone. He gave the slightest toss of his old head.

"That way, yes. Thank you," Zero told him in passing, keeping to the edge of the wall. The warmount had chosen his battleground and Zero felt confident the old horse would hold the rear approach to the hospice. Something flashed through the air ahead making a sound like tearing cloth, followed almost instantly by a tremendous flare of red lightning and a cracking boom which made Zero crouch even lower to the stones.

Zero's sense of Geoffrey's presence flickered, then steadied, but weaker now. Zero wished he could have been closer to tell his squire not to put so much of his essence into his arrows, but it wasn't something he'd been expecting the young necroknight to be able to manifest so early after his creation. Or by using his bow. It was a rare enough ability even when channeled through a sword.

The human guardians of Invercraig had cowered under that terrible blast as well, but they were also moving forward again, earning Zero's admiration for their bravery in the face of unknown magick. The mixed force of human and free undead met the Risen ghouls on the burnside path and backyards of the village and a great slaughter began.

There were still enough ghouls left after Geoffrey's lightning to worry Zero. "Rally to me!" he yelled, igniting his sword to a visible blue glow. "Invercraig! Geoffrey!"

He hated making a target of himself, but sometimes it was that or watch his companions get picked off. He joined a pair of women wielding axes, cleaving the head off a ghoul armed with a highland claymore.

The women flinched away from his sword, but he bellowed, "Invercraig!" at them before they turned their axes on him. Recognizing the necroknight, they joined up on his flanks. Together they rushed up to where two old men were fighting back to back against four ghouls and started hacking.

Five against four swung the odds back in favor of the villagers. "Stay together!" Zero ordered them after the last ghoul dropped. He sprinted off to intercept another pair of ghouls trying to skulk down the burnside and bypass the scattered combats to get into the town.

The ghouls had finesse and knew how to fight as a pair. Zero had finesse of his own from years of fighting. Added to that, he had a necroknight's greater strength and speed. And he had his arcane skills, just as devastating in their way as Geoffrey's blast of red lightning.

He stunned the ghouls by pulling warmth and magick out of the very air around them and moved in with sword and the blackthorn club. The two ghouls barely slowed him down.

Then he was running back up the path, putting his weapons into Risen bodies, putting them through spines and cracking off skulls in passing as he fought his way to where Geoffrey was running down his own foes, beyond the charred pieces of those he'd dropped lightning on.

The more experienced among the ghouls had realized they were facing an enraged necroknight and were attempting an orderly retreat. That retreat shattered when Zero arrived to cover his squire, pulling what warmth he could out of the air and rock on a larger scale and causing frost to form over the largest remaining cluster of Risen. It wouldn't kill them, but it made moving more painful and difficult.

Geoffrey put one of the blackthorn arrows into the ghoul who'd been acting as commander. It keened in pain and staggered, but didn't go down immediately.

"Geoffrey?" Zero suggested mildly, "I think those will work better on the living."

Geoffrey blinked several times. "Arrows against undead, what am I thinking?" he asked. He still didn't seem quite recovered from the berserker burst of anger and frustration which had sent lightning into the Risen once already. The sparks of small lightnings were beginning to discharge around his hands and arms.

Zero'd seen that madness in battle before and hip-checked his squire. "Hey! Focus! Ground that before you drop it on your own head!"

Geoffrey snarled and spun with him, discarding the bow for the hand axe Zero had given him.

"Oh, hells!" Zero growled, but at least he had the young necroknight's attention. He shifted his grip on the blackthorn club and managed to snag hold of one of Geoffrey's chainmail sleeves keeping his enraged companion from doing more than smacking him with the flat of the axe blade, rather than the edge. With his other hand, he swung his sword toward the now paused and confused group of Risen ghouls at the same time. Squeezing his eyes shut in expectation of what was about to happen, he drew on the remaining dampness in the air, making a link between the Risen and himself just in time.

Red lightning tore open the air between them, searing over Zero and scattering pieces of Risen from where the lightning finally grounded. Geoffrey fell to his knees, pulling out of Zero's stunned grasp, and then collapsed entirely onto the ground, smoldering.

Deafened, singed, and almost blind despite having closed his eyes, Zero charged the remaining Risen, screaming.

Even for undead, this was entirely too much. Skeletons and true zombies wouldn't have run, simply because they didn't have enough minds left to recognize their final deaths approaching at speed. Ghouls could think for themselves and lacking an immediate leader, they scattered. Or scattered as best they could, between the cliff and the water.

Several went into the water. The rest ran up the path.

Zero ran down the ones on the path, sucking up what remained of their animating force as he slew them, one by one. Finally, nothing moved before him and he slowed down.

He probed the night ahead of him, feeling only the faintest of life beginning to seep up from the roots of trees and bushes. If the necromancer from the night before had sent the ghouls, that necromancer hadn't remained to see what the attack accomplished.

Zero sighed and started jogging back. Every inch hurt, but he needed to get back to the village. He needed to make certain either Geoffrey was truly dead or be there to steady and restrain his squire as he recovered. And to see if there would even be time for it or if Invercraig had also been assaulted from other directions.

A voice from the waterside challenged him, "What be ye on the burnside path?"

"What be ye?" Zero echoed, bringing his sword on guard.

A clatter like small stones rattling together sounded and something walked up to the edge of the path, heavy with the scent of seaweed and rot. "T'h!" exclaimed the creature in disappointment on seeing Zero. "Dead-alive, but one of ours. Was it you who sent me those tasty snacks for my larder?"

"Some of them, milady," Zero said, bowing cautiously with both arms spread, but still holding his weapons, and his eyes never leaving the shellycoat's face. "More by the villagers of Invercraig."

"Yes," the water fay smiled toothily. "I'll eat well this year. You needn't worry about those who sullied my waters just now. Impolite whelps thinking they could go splashing though my territory without leaving a gift. They'll not be bothering you dry-landers again." She undulated in a graceful stretch and tilted her head at him in thoughtful examination. "Would you care to come dine with me, handsome boy?"

There was an offer he didn't often receive since he'd been turned. Anxious as he was to get back to his squire and the town, he still bowed again, more deeply this time. “I would be delighted, milady, but I have given my word to aid and protect those in the village now. And the night is not yet safe for them.”

“Wisely said and well. Though you may tell them for the turning of the year’s wheel ‘til this season comes again, I consider they have paid their dues to me and mine. We will be one less thing for them to fear in the dark waters until then. Perhaps if they continue to send such feasting, such an arrangement could last?”

“Perhaps,” said Zero. “I will tell them, but it is not my decision to make. However,” he pointed up the path. “There are more dead ghouls that way, if you’d like to harvest them.”

The shellycoat’s toothy smile widened and she turned toward the burn again. “Perhaps, no. Perhaps, yes,” she said, unclearly as to whether she was speaking of the villagers or of gathering the dead bodies. “We will see what the season brings, Sir Knight.”

She turned back fully at the edge of the burn, now a green-tressed beauty in a gown of seasilk trimmed with bright shells and gleaming stones. “Good hunting to you, Sir.”

“And to you, Lady of the Craigburn and of other waters, good hunting.”

She disappeared under the water of the stream and Zero hurried the rest of the way back to where he’d left Geoffrey lying.

Broken Sky stood over him, watching, while the villagers of Invercraig hurriedly tended their wounded and gathered their dead. The warmount nosed Geoffrey’s feebly twitching body, then looked pointedly at Zerollen.

“If I do, I hope you know where we’ll feed, old man.”

The old horse turned his head, one eye toward Zero, the other toward Geoffrey. Then he raised his upper lip and wiggled it around in horsey laughter before giving himself a good full-body shake.

"On your head then," said Zero, kneeling beside the warmount's great hooves where they were keeping Geoffrey pinned to the ground. "I thought you'd chosen a rider?"

Broken Sky laughed again and waggled his ears, finishing with a nose bunt to Zero's back.

"Behave, you great beast," Zero scolded. "This isn't as easy as it looks."

Geoffrey thrashed then, snapping his teeth, but Broken Sky held him down.

"You behave, as well," Zero told him, but more gently. "Steady. I'll have you feeling better in just a few moments, Geoff."

Necroknights hadn't been created with healing in mind, but they could share energy, particularly between a knight and their squire. Warmounts shared a similar bond with their riders. Certainly, if Bessariel had been there, Zero would have expected her to anchor him. That Broken Sky was willing to aid him came as a surprise. Then again, the old warmount had chosen a living rider and a child at that, so surprises seemed something to almost be expected from him.

The easiest way to share energy was to share blood. It was also one of the more dangerous ways to do it, depending on the strength of the knight receiving the blood. Zero shrugged and punctured one of the veins on the back of his hand with the knife he kept in his boot, then held his hand deliberately to Geoffrey's snapping mouth.

"Agah!" he cried out as Geoff savaged his hand, but Broken Sky brought his head to Zero's shoulder and a warmth spread from the warmount to the necroknight like being enfolded within a great heated cloak. It was so unexpected and surprising, he almost fell on top of Geoffrey, barely catching himself with his uninjured knife hand before he did.

The mad flicker of red lighting in the younger necroknight's eyes faded to violet, deepened back into purple, and finally, the familiar arcane blue. Geoff blinked in surprise, quickly followed by a certain dawning horror. He released Zero's hand, pulling away as much as he could with Broken Sky pinning him to the ground by his clothing and armor, grimacing even as his body demanded the last few tastes of blood still on his lips. Zero pulled back as well, cradling his mangled hand, almost in tears as the warmth which had suffused him slipped away.

The warmount lifted his head and stepped off of Geoffrey with delicate care. He took three long steps away, then folded his legs, and settled to a patch of unsullied ground with a groan.

Both necroknights watched Broken Sky with concern before Geoff turned his attention again to Zero. "You came back," he said, voice thick with emotion.

Zero reached out and squeezed Geoff's arm with his good hand. "Couldn't leave you like that after you saved us all," he said. "That would have been damned ungrateful."

Geoffrey smiled wearily. "Dyer wasn't with them."

"We'll get him. And that damned resurrectionist as well." Zero fumbled the pot of green healing paste out of a pocket. Together they managed to get the lid open, the fresh green scent of the contents steadying both of them.

"This will hurt," warned Zero. And he rubbed some of it over Geoffrey's bitten lips and scorched face. His squire moaned and writhed as the salve did its work, but didn't lash out again. When Geoff had recovered, Zero stripped off what was left of his squire's gloves and coated his burnt hands as carefully as he could. Geoffrey cried out and thrashed and almost slashed his lips again before the pain passed.

He perked up a bit more as the pain eased, focusing suddenly on something over Zero's shoulder. It caused the senior knight to jerk around in alarm to see what Geoff was looking at.

It was Hector, setting a bucket on top of the wall. He dove out of sight for a moment and reappeared with a quilt he threw onto the wall as well.

Zero unsteadily climbed to his feet and helped Geoffrey stand up. The younger necroknight wobbled a bit, but followed Zero over to the boy. "Water for all of you," Hector told them, climbing over the wall, "but mostly for Broken Sky. And this to warm him."

After Geoffrey and Zero both drank deeply, they helped the boy carry the bucket to the warmount.

Broken Sky was frighteningly still with his nose pushed into the ground. Hector wrapped his arms around his mount's neck, whispering in his ears. After a few moments the old beast roused enough to drink. Zero wondered if the pot of green paste would help and carefully offered the old horse some; Broken Sky mouthed a finger's scoop of the ointment, refusing more. Zero and Geoffrey spread the quilt over his back. After a few minutes of Hector curled against his head, stroking him, the old warmount let them know he wanted to get up. With Zero and Geoff steadying him on either side, he staggered to his feet. After a few minutes more, the four of them walked slowly down to the south gate.

Zero didn't want to leave them, but something nagged at him as being unfinished. "There's something I have to do yet. I'll join you up at the Great House." He gave Geoff a look, commanding, "No more lightning."

Geoffrey cracked a wry smile. "Not even if it's Dyer?"

Broken Sky reached around slowly, but with great deliberateness and grabbed one of Geoffrey's elbows between his teeth. And squeezed.

"God's ba—ha! Beard. Not even if it *is* Dyer, then."

"Don't go undoing what he just did for you," said Hector, smacking Geoff with his cap.

"I won't. I won't! Promise!"

Zero smiled and left them at the gate, walking back to the battleground while still holding his Geoffrey-bitten hand to kept it from bumping against anything. The vicar was arguing with someone about not having time to bless or burn the dead. "Have you found all of your people?" Zero asked, breaking in on the argument.

"We have," said the young vicar, stiffly.

"Good." Zero continued past the humans to where the first of Geoffrey's lightning bolts had fallen.

The vicar, the person he'd been arguing with, and several others had followed him. "What are you planning on doing?" demanded the vicar.

Zero gave him a side-eyed glance. "Making sure they won't be raised again by whatever sent them in the first place. And healing my hand."

Before anyone could protest, Zero sent tendrils of necromantic energy seeking similar traces. Little pools of energy responded and he pulled on them through his tracers. "Get up!" he commanded. "What of ye that can, get up!"

"What in God's Name do you think you're doing?" shrieked the young vicar, backing away as things twitched on the ground and some stood up again. Startled exclamations came from other villagers.

Purple-black and blue-purple wisps like thin fog were already forming in the air above and around the bodies and flowing toward Zero, winding up his legs and torso. Zero tilted his head at the vicar and his frightened companions, his eyes now aglow with blue-purple light. “This,” he said and made a sudden grasping, wrenching gesture with his injured hand.

The things which had stood up and the things twitching on the ground stopped. The standing ones fell. More purple wisps flew through the air or rolled across the ground and wrapped around Zero, vanishing into his body. And the torn flesh and crushed and shattered bones knit back together as he bent around his hand from the pain of the healing.

Zero hissed through his teeth as the last of the necromantic energy infused him. He flexed his hand and wiggled his now only-bruised fingers. “Nothing will bring them back now without making quite a fight of it,” he said, starting toward Invercraig. “Whether they are burnt or not.”

He walked back into the village and no one got in his way.

7: SCOUTING PARTIES

Zero caught up with Geoffrey, Hector, and Broken Sky on the far side of the village and helped them escort the exhausted warmount up the twisty road to the Great House. Both Hector and his mount were quickly co-opted to help the stable master and her daughter keep the rest of the town's horses and other stock from bolting back to their stalls and byres in the village. At least until other villagers had made some last hasty repairs to the old fences and gates. Broken Sky was surprisingly effective at this by simply standing by the pasture fence and showing his teeth to the horses and other critters. The two necroknights left Hector there to watch over Broken Sky and headed back to the village to check on the evacuation.

Villagers were coming and going down the road. Most still didn't seem concerned about the necroknights in their midst. But some of the ones coming up from Invercraig squished themselves as close to the inner side of the road as they could get from the pair.

"Well, fuck," said Zero, clenching and unclenching the hand Geoffrey had bitten.

"What's with that?" Geoffrey asked, eyes on the villagers. "Did I suddenly grow two heads?

"Might as well have," said Zero.

"Hm, some of the ones who saw what I did?"

"And what I did, after you fell. And moreso after when I cleaned up the dead we didn't have time to burn."

Geoff looked at him askance, noticing the purple tendrils still waving around his companion like vines seeking a support. "What did you *do*, Zerollen?"

"Full name, is it?" Zero rolled an eye at Geoff. "Well, I supposed what I did deserves that level of rebuke. I raised the ghouls as mindless and then took that animating force back into myself. It's not quite as thorough as burning, but it would take quite a lot to animate them again. Only a greater resurrectionist could do it and there's really no point in wasting that much energy just for mindless undead. Someone would have to be desperate *and* have more power than's good for anyone."

"You can do that?" Geoffrey seemed both curious and stricken.

"I can animate dead," Zero corrected, looking down at the weather-damaged road. "Yes, but not as much as people would think. Most of what I can affect has to have been tainted already. Normal humans don't usually linger long after they die to get caught. I likely got you back only because you were already tainted and would have risen on your own."

Zero paused a moment at the gate and recovered the rolled and burr- and blood-covered blanket cloak he'd hidden when he first cleared the village. One never knew when extra cloth for bandages might keep someone alive. And he didn't want whatever of his own blood might still be on it to be found by an enemy. He found his original hat as well, tangled in the cloth and whin.

The pair of necroknights walked down the road and back into Invercraig, which was emptying quickly. At the hospice, women were carrying out the last of the children and loading them into a wagon. Goody Greneglais came out of her house carrying several sacks and set them behind the seat. She nodded to the two of them.

Then she went to where her sign still glowed softly and did something her body blocked from their sight. When she turned back, she carried the carved staff with her and the light came with it.

She took her seat beside the driver on the wagon. The driver clucked to her team and shook the reins and the horses stepped forward, leaning just enough into their collars to get the wagon moving. Bannock looked up from where he was curled between Aggie and Mary-wee. Zero and Geoffrey flanked the wagon. Along with the last of the villagers, they set out for the Great House.

Zero and Geoffrey peeled off where the road up to the Great House split from the coastal road. The evacuation had gone surprisingly well. Once the last wagons passed, some of the villagers were rolling rocks across the Great House road to make a barricade.

Watching them, Zero had a sudden realization. "Geoffrey, how many rode with you?"

"Close to a full hundred company when we left Invar Nis," said Geoff. "But we started getting sick almost as soon as we got out of the city. We were something less than four score when we got to the farm. And I've seen better than half that dead, if you ran down all the ghouls I missed in the latest attack. I'm not certain all of those were from my company either."

Zero gave him a bleak stare. "Buggery. That's still too many if they all come back at once. Especially if they come back as Risen."

"That's what I thought as well," said Geoffrey. "The Great House is defensible, but it has some serious weak spots, especially if they can get close enough to climb."

The two of them started trotting up to the Great House. "We need to find out where the rest of them are and if that resurrectionist caught all of them."

***

"No, you can't," said the stable master. She gestured at her charges, the horses and other equines of Invercraig. "Not when I can still see purple death dripping off of you. If you go, you're going to have to go on foot."

Zero growled, but he couldn't really argue, not with Broken Sky shaking his head at him from behind her, his ears laid back. And not with still visible tendrils of purple-black twining around his boots, either. The herd was already shifting nervously just with him nearby.

"I guess I'll walk," he said to Geoffrey.

"Better you both walk," said a voice. The spectral Laird of Craig House manifested enough to be heard and seen. "And stay together."

"Something we should know, milaird?"

The old laird shook his ghostly head. "Just practicality. The two of you are stronger together. You'd be stronger if the horse could go with you, but no one can force a horse like that. And he's pushing his boundaries as it is." The specter faded into the shadows, but his voice stayed with them, "Stay together. Search to the north. Between myself and our fay neighbors, no attackers will come through Invercraig easily."

Both necroknights looked around, but the laird neither reappeared nor added to his commands.

"Well, then," Geoffrey shook his head. "Sounds like we have our orders."

"What orders?" asked Hector coming down to the courtyard bailey with a steaming bucket he took over to Broken Sky. Zero caught a whiff of warm bran as the warmount eagerly jammed his nose into the bucket.

"I don't recall having given you atrocities any orders," said an ancient old human male who had appeared at the top of the stairs leading up to the great hall. "But you need to make yourselves useful and get to work on fortifying this place, if you're going to be staying here."

Zero gave the stranger a curious and annoyed look. "I don't recall having ever met you before. I don't recall having even seen you. And you call me an atrocity and then have the colossal nerve to try ordering me and my squire about?"

"I am a Deacon of the Church and of the Guild of Shipwrights," thundered the old man, clearly offended. "And you will submit to God's Will and obey your betters!"

"Zero," warned Geoffrey. "Mind where those seekers of yours are going. They're damn cold."

"Grandfather!" someone yelled from inside the hall.

"Deacon Fraiser!" yelled another, familiar voice at the same time.

Zero ignored the elderly deacon and was pulling his 'seekers' as Geoffrey had named them, back into himself. When he looked up again, Alasdair MacIver had appeared beside the old man, as he was about halfway down the stairs toward the two necroknights. "Deacon! You be leavin' Zero diGriz and his squire out of your ranting!"

"I'll mind you to keep your nose out of my business, Alasdair MacIver, you old heathen! There's spars to be lifting."

Several women came out after Alasdair, seemingly divided between capturing, supporting, or otherwise intercepting their elders. A small crowd of the folks trying to care for and securely pen the livestock were also looking up or gathering on the edges of the courtyard.

And it began raining again.

"We should be going," suggested Geoffrey.

"Before this gets any more crowded and ridiculous," Zero agreed. "Hector! Broken Sky! Stay safe!"

"You'll come back?" asked the boy, rather forlornly.

"We'll be back," Zero promised. "Take care of yourself and your sisters until then."

"You leave now and you can just keep going, you undead traitors!" roared the deacon from somewhere inside the group trying to get him back into the hall.

"Is it always like this?" asked Geoffrey as they walked away.

"Oh, sometimes there's torches and pitchforks," Zero replied. "At least Bannock didn't run out and bite me on the leg this time and no one's throwing rotten turnips at us."

No one else objected when they said they were going out scouting. Soon they were back on the coastal road, walking north with the steep mountainside on one hand and the north channel on the other just beyond the verge and startlingly white sand. It would have been a pleasant walk but for the rain. Not far up the coastal road, the mountain spur pushed into the sea, sliced through with a narrow steep-sided cut with sides so glossy and smooth they had to have been laid back by a mage with engineering skills or a team of dwarves.

"Except for the lack of cover, we could hold quite a number here," said Geoffrey.

"We could slow them down, even so," agreed Zero. "But it wouldn't end well for us. We'd need at least a few more fighters and a squad of archers would be nice. Heh, not likely to happen. There's an old temple to Nyorth just up the coast. We'll go as far as that and then start back."

Beyond the narrows, the tillable land spread out and old farmsteads were visible, though little of it looked to be worked. Several farms seemed to have had some plowing done, but all of those were closest to the narrows. Beyond them, uncut grasses, brush and small trees covered fields which seemed years fallow, except for some grazing.

"What happened here?" asked Geoffrey, startled to see what looked like decent farming land so abandoned.

"The Risen Tsar marched on Tir na Scota and Tir na n'Alba for their treasures," said Zero. "And on Scotland as well, before pushing on to Eireland and Tir na n'Eire. Have you never been so far north before, Geoffrey?"

The younger necroknight shook his head. "I'd not been to the Borders until Dyer led us north. I think he was looking for a place like this, where he could take land and set himself up as a ruler with no one to dispute his claim. I think that must have been what he saw with Invercraig. Maybe he even knew the town and the keep were up here – he's a Scot. Maybe it was where we'd been heading since leaving Angland. But he changed as we rode north. What he did, leaving me dead or dying at the MacLeans? What he let be done in Invercraig? That wasn't the man I'd taken service with. Something changed him, but it happened so slowly, I didn't see it, until I was too sick to protest."

"Were you one of his officers?"

"No, just one of the regulars."

"Well, then, about all you might have done was take your pay and ride out. Or start an insurrection."

"Hm, I wonder about that. Seeing what I saw, most of the decent ones were the first to sicken. Maybe that puts me in better company?"

Zero grinned and gave him a sly look from under the brim of his hat. "It certainly does now."

Geoff snorted. "Seriously, Zero, what sort of disease sickens the better folk first? I've seen plague strike down whole towns, it isn't picky."

"Likewise." Zero thought about it for a bit as they walked. "What if it had help? What if you were poisoned?"

"Poisoned?

"Had there been sickness in Invar Nis while you were there?"

Geoffrey considered the question. "No, nothing I remember hearing. And we weren't staying near the docks, though some of the men could have brought it up from there with the doxies they frequented."

"There are the ruins of Nyorth's temple," said Zero, pointing out several dark, irregular shapes silhouetted against the sea in the distance. "And I smell a wood fire. Someone's burning pine off that way." He gestured inland. "Let's go see what's over there."

Over there turned out to be an abandoned farm's woodlot where three humans had made a camp for the night.

Two men seemed to be sleeping on branches of fresh cut pine next to a large stone, close to where the radiant heat from a stacked fire mostly hidden by a slightly smaller rock and a clever screen of more pine branches could warm them. The third was keeping guard and occasionally adding a small log or large dead branch to the top of the stack.

"I know those men," Geoffrey told Zero, after they had watched the camp for some time. "Merryweather Steward, Long Tom Brown, and Toby of Wessex."

"Good men or ill?"

"I would have said no worse than me and likely better."

"Think they'd talk to us?"

"They might. Merryweather was a friend."

Careful scouting had turned up no one else anywhere close by. "Can't hurt to try," Zero decided. "Maybe we can learn something. At the least, we'll see how they'll react to us."

He stood from where he'd been crouching and started walking toward the light. "Hullo the camp!" he called.

"Hullo!" The one Geoffrey had identified as Merryweather started and kept to the shelter of the pines. "Come forward and be recognized."

Zero could hear him rousing the sleepers while they approached.

"That's close enough. Who are you?"

"Might as well cut to the chase right away," Geoffrey said softly to Zero, then continued loud enough to carry to his former comrades. "You know me, Merry Steward."

"Geoff? Dyer said you'd deserted, but we thought you surely dead of the sickness," said one of the other two men.

"And you weren't far wrong," said Geoff. "Dyer left me for dead."

"So," Merryweather drew the word out. "I'm thinking you didn't just show up to collect gambling debts. Who's your friend?"

"Zerollen diGriz," Zero introduced himself before Geoff might have used that annoying 'sir' before his name.

"The road agent?" asked Merryweather in surprise. "Hells, there are songs about you."

"Former road agent," Zero corrected. "And don't believe everything you've heard from minstrels."

"What about that most recent one? The one about you being a free undead?"

Zero couldn't help it, he grimaced. "That one's partly true," he admitted.

"Geoffrey?" Merryweather asked, a pleading tone entering his voice.

Geoffrey nodded. "Me too. Zero's told me I was already tainted and likely to have Risen even if he hadn't stumbled across me."

"Fuck!" said the three men in unison.

"And I supposed that resurrectionist sent you after us then?" asked Merry, now several shades paler even in the faint firelight.

"Hells, no!" snapped Geoff.

"We're hunting that one," Zero added.

"Damn," said Merry. "Okay. You weren't sent by Dyer or the resurrectionist. Then what *are* you doing out here in the middle of nowhere on foot? Don't you have warhorses or something?"

"Warmounts. And they're otherwise occupied. What are *you* doing out here?"

"Running from undead, curiously enough. And trying to decide where to go next."

"Why aren't you with Dyer?"

"Because. Answer the first, he'd gone over the bounds when we took that little village back the road." Merryweather gestured in a vaguely southern direction that encompassed the farms and Invercraig. "And answer the second, because he and most of what's left of the company are either undead now or in service with the resurrectionist."

"You could have led off with that one," said Geoffrey.

Zero was about to ask more when he noticed all the horses suddenly swing their heads around and stare out into the dark.

"Something's coming," he warned.

When the others turned to see what the horses had spooked at, he murmured, "No lightning," to Geoff and stepped off into the darkness.

A dozen ghouls came bounding through the fields, one running on all fours with its head down like a hunting hound. Zero moved to intercept them, keeping to the shelter of the pines. As they closed on the small camp, three quickly released arrows found their marks, but only one of the ghouls fell and did not rise again. Horses screamed in panic and pulled the picket line loose, only to get tangled among the pines. Men and ghouls met and much hacking and biting began.

These ghouls ran without weapons and only a few wore armor. Zero came in from the side with his sword and the blackthorn club. Long Tom and Merryweather fought back-to-back like a long-practiced team. Toby put his back to the rocks and hewed about himself with a pair of wicked axes. Geoffrey fell back and sent arrows into the ghouls from close range, using the broad-headed hunting arrows he'd been able to scavenge to surprisingly good effect before joining the hand-to-hand fighting with his mace and the handaxe Zero had given him.

The fight was vicious, but mostly silent, except for the squeals of the panicked horses.

When it was over, the impromptu group found themselves mostly unharmed but for a few minor slashes. Zero scanned as far out as he could send his seekers, but found no more and no one who might have sent them.

"Now what?" asked Merryweather after the horses were calmed and untangled, while Toby bound up his and Long Tom's cuts.

"I'd take you back to Invercraig with us, but with the excitement our going on patrol caused and that some of the villagers might recognize you? I think the best thing you can do is ride north and spread the alarm. If we're very lucky, you might intercept my warmount and a few Caliburn knights coming this way. Let people know Invercraig will likely need all the help it can get, if they can spare anyone to aid us."

Zero gave them a very hard stare, adding, "Find a priest or whatever you call your holy people and get those wounds purified so you don't take rot or worse from those bites."

The former raiders left to ride north and Zero and Geoff dragged the bodies of the re-dead into the pines and lit them after chopping off heads, sending a blaze towering above the copse of pine in warning to any who might see it.

Then they ran for Invercraig and the Great House.

"We'll check the farms which looked inhabited. I want no one and nothing living which we could herd back to Invercraig left out unprotected with a host of Risen prowling this way."

Cutting across the fields, they found a feisty ram who only veered off from charging them at the last moment. Despite Zero's best intentions, the beast was too nasty and too quick to herd without a dog.

Further along, approaching a bothy, they woke a flock of geese who would give even a pack of ghouls pause. A goose girl - human, not a shapeshifter - came out of the bothy and berated them for trying to steal a goose.

"No! Woman! For the Gods' sakes, there are Risen about and reavers and a resurrectionist. We're pulling everyone back to Craig House for protection. For the Gods' Sakes, you stupid creatures, stop that!" Zero swiped at some of the geese with his club, but they dodged out of the way as though practiced at such maneuvers.

"Looks like the Risen are already here," said the girl and started to close the door.

"No, the bad one—" Geoffrey started. "The other bad ones, then."

"The ones that will eat you," Zero offered. "And your bitey geese. And anything else they can get their teeth on."

"There were reavers through already," said the girl, doubtfully.

"And likely to be coming back, either as men or as ghouls, I know not which," said Zero. "May Lugh and Cian witness, I promise no harm will come to you and any of your kin from me or my squire if you will let us get you safely to Craig House where the village of Invercraig now shelters."

"What about my geese?"

"I'm seriously reserving judgement on these geese." The geese were big enough to kill a man if they'd been wild. They likely still could, though technically tame. Zero was tolerating them only because they had a certain leeriness of humans and beings shaped like humans.

"Well, I can't really blame you for that," she said as another goose tried to bite Zero. "I'll get my carry bag. Back off and let me get the flock gathered."

Zero and Geoffrey backed off. The geese pursued until the goose girl came out and gathered them, moving them with a long stick. They didn't want to move particularly well and kept trying to settle for the night, but by keeping a rather loose formation and with many orders from the goose girl, they got the gaggle moving back to the girl's home, a small but tidy cottage. Once there, they let the geese settle into their pen. The girl, whose name was Chritiana, roused her mother and explained the danger. Complaints quickly turned to commands on what to gather from outside the cot. In a surprisingly short time, they had a handcart padded with the family bed and sheets, their crippled grandmother nested within with other of the family treasures. With Zero pushing the cart and mother, daughter, and Geoffrey herding the very grumpy geese they were able to leave the fields for a farm lane which made for somewhat smoother and faster travel. No humans were at the next farm they came to, but an old cranky donkey wandered out to meet them from a nearby field and, while avoiding the humans and necroknights, added itself to the gaggle without provoking the irritable birds.

Most of the remaining farms they needed to check were off the lane they were now following which made things easier. The rests while Zero or Geoffrey ranged out to sweep more distant sheds or bothies gave the geese time to forage and the stone fences and hedges along the lane kept them mostly funneled in the direction they needed to go. The MacLaines also knew which steadings were being worked and where holdouts were likely to have stayed.

They picked up an old couple with their pony and cart, dogs, and a small flock of sheep, which actually made moving the geese easier with the dogs to turn them back when they tried to scatter. To that, they added another youth with a small mixed group of geese and ducks and thanked the Gods waterfowl would normally move around at night. “This is why chickens go to market in crates,” observed Chritiana’s mother.

They were almost back to the coastal road and the Narrows when noise and light at the farm closest to Invercraig drew everyone’s attention. “Jean MacKintosh’s daughter Marsali was in childbed,” said old Maeve MacLaine. “Looks like the bairn picked a bad time for birthin.”

Zero and Geoffrey crept up on the farmhouse to find three armored ghouls trying to pry a shutter loose from the building while a fourth gave orders. Or at least it gave orders up until Zero soft-footed up behind it and put one of his knives into its eye socket. It went down, flopping and kicking, but drew the attention of the three trying to force the shutter. Zero was left fending them off with sword and dagger until Geoffrey came in from the other side and smashed one’s face in with his mace and took out the knees on another. Zero got knocked back with a hastily grabbed shield. But the ghoul hadn’t had time to don it securely; the shield was twisted out of its hand and went flying with Zero, but so did Zero’s sword.

The small necroknight pulled up the blackthorn club and scuttled crabwise to his sword. The ghoul charged over and kicked it away.

Zero tangled the ghoul’s legs with the blackthorn’s long handle and pushed back, tripping the ghoul who had swiped at him with a mace of its own.

Zero made it to his feet first and brought the blackthorn club down on the ghoul, crunching into its shoulder. The ghoul connected with his mace, but without much strength behind the blow. Then Geoffrey had fought his way through and stove in the ghoul's nose guard and smashed most of its face. Zero finished it with his dirk.

"They're a lot nastier with armor on," Geoff commented, giving Zero a hand up.

"That they are," said Zero. "You okay?"

"Bruises. Nothing serious."

"If you go get our parade, I'll deal with these."

Zero dragged the dead behind one of the outbuildings where neither the humans they'd already rescued or the people in the house would be able to see what he was doing. As he had in Invercraig, he raised the freshly dead ghouls, then pulled all of the animating force back out of them. That done, he went through their pockets, then stripped off their armor and collected it in a pile to which he added their weapons.

While the MacLaines and the other MacLaines – Maeve MacLaine had been married to Tam MacLaine's brother Johnny – convinced the MacKintoshes to come out and gather their livestock, Zero and Geoff found their wagon and rolled it out of its shed. Geoff also caught their chickens and crated them. The goose-herding MacLaines got the horses hitched and the MacKintoshes' four cows moving along with the geese and the donkey. Crated hens, several cheeses, and a side of beef were loaded, along with beds and blankets, the two recently birthed babies - one of the dairymaids had also had a son - and their mothers, family treasures, and a very pleased herding dog bitch who was in the midst of having her litter. Tam MacLaine added his sheep to the oddly mixed herd and everyone got moving again. Zero slipped off to the fringes of the activity, searching the darkness for more ghouls, but nothing else seemed to be moving.

The MacKintoshes were the last of the holdouts and somehow even with geese, sheep, cows, and a donkey in the dark and the rain, they got the whole lot safely up to Craig House where the humans and their babes and the birthing hound and her litter were hurried into the great hall to get warmed and sorted out. The donkey and the geese and ducks with their brave young people still herding them were added into the pens of sleepy complaining critters. Tam MacLaine and the MacKintoshes' cowherd got the cows and sheep confined. Finally, all of the humans were done penning animals and they and the necroknights could make their way into the hall and get warm.

The old bartender from the Salmon was up and directed what few adults remained awake. The goose girl and the duck boy were dried off, fed, and sent to join her mother and grandmother with the other MacLaines. The MacKintoshes found their kin. Then the old woman, two of the MacIvers, and the acting head of the town council began questioning Zero and Geoffrey about what they'd seen.

"The most disturbing thing," Zero finished up his report. "None of the ghouls we fought at first were armed. A few had some remnants of armor, but it was as much getting in their way as protecting them. It wasn't until we'd reached the MacKintosh farm that we found recently risen ghouls with useful arms and armor and there were only four of them."

"At least you got a warning going north. If those men can get through to the next town without Dyer's Company intercepting them. Between them and you setting that copse of pine on fire, you did what you could to spread the word. And maybe bring us relief, if the undead lay siege."

The council head added, "We've got some boats out as well. With luck, they'll have reached safe harbors up or down the coast and be spreading the word to other as might come help us."

"I don't know if you two actually sleep, but you look like you need it. Rest here and get warm again. We'll likely need your help all too soon."

Rest was a tempting thought, but neither of them were willing to stop moving until they'd peeked in on where Aggie and Mary-wee were sleeping with the other ill or slowly recovering patients. Goody Greneglais was asleep in a chair near them, while one of her helpers snored on the floor and another kept watch.

Finally satisfied, the two knights propped themselves near the door and just waited for the morning, which was already and all too soon arriving.

"What would you like to do, provided we survive the next couple of days?"

"I think I'd like to find a sunny hillside and just sit there and watch my horse graze," said Zero. "At least until the insides of my bones are warm again."

"Sounds good to me," said Geoffrey. "Maybe stay here and raise MacLeans, at least until Hector reaches his majority and takes a wife or Aggie takes a husband."

Zero chuckled. "Raising little humans and farming, there's something you don't see necroknights doing every day. There's something rather appealing about it. At least as long as they don't get sick again. I'm not anxious to go back to playing nurse anytime soon."

8: FIRST ENCOUNTERS

They moved back outside when the sun rose. On the edge of the crag where bits of the outer wall still stood, they found a spot where they could see north to beyond the Narrows and south into the village as the morning fog burned off. They stayed there, enjoying the early sun and being out of everyone else's way until mid-morning.

Healer Greneglais and another of the town councilors joined them then, the healer bringing steaming mugs of a tisane which had some of the same smell as the ointment she'd gifted Zero with before he'd gone to rescue the children. Both necroknights drank gratefully.

"Nothing's appeared out of the fog. We've not seen any movement in the town or out in the dale beyond the Narrows."

"Could they come up the crag?" asked the councilor, a grizzled woman missing a leg below the knee. "I saw ghouls scale some unlikely climbs in the Low Countries."

"Nothing's impossible," said Zero. "I've not seen the back of the crag or explored the mountain. Was the House ever assaulted that way?"

"Not in my memory, though I wasn't here when the Risen came through, so I don't know what they did to take the House." She gave Zero a hard look. "I don't suppose you remember anything about it?"

"I was further north at the defense of Thornhill and Tir na Scota. I fell before they pushed into the Hidden Roads," Zero said without taking offense, but with a touch of evasiveness. "When I remember anything clearly again, I was in the Russ and Tercel Davidson and the Caliburn Knights had just freed a number of us."

"I suspect it'll depend on whether Dyer thinks of sending anyone up," said Geoffrey. "If he can still think. Merryweather told me they'd seen a necromancer with the main company."

"Which reminds me, Geoff," said Zero. "Did the company have any spellslingers you'd forgotten to mention before now?"

"No one in holy orders would ride with us. And Dyer hates mages with a passion, so none of them either. We did have a decent number of mounted archers, though nothing like the Hunnish have."

"You rode with Dyer's Company?" asked Healer Greneglais, startled.

"We hadn't really gotten to discussing how I ended up like this, had we?" Geoff looked away as though embarrassed, then back. "Yes, I was with them. I took sick sometime before we reached the MacLean farm. Zero found me floating in their spring."

"Oh! Oh, that's terrible. They'd just left you there?"

"I think I was searching for water. I likely fell in and drowned. I don't remember and that's probably God's blessing. Someone could just as easily have pushed me in and held me under." Geoff's eyes sparked paler to a violet shade reminiscent of the red lightning he'd called the night before. "If someone did, I think I'll give them a good surprise when we meet again."

"Indeed, sir," said the councilor in the silence that briefly fell across them. "And I, for one, would blame you not at all. Now, I need must go speak with others about how to best arrange our stores and defenses. We'll meet later to further plan, if we have that time."

But they didn't get that time, for just before noon riders appeared in the farming dale and came trotting toward Invercraig.

"If we had more archers, we could have made a stand there," said Geoff. "But there's no way we could have covered a retreat. Damn that the cut stone and walls were pulled down for building elsewhere. Hunting arrows aren't going to stop them."

"No, but we can roll rocks down on them. We've still plenty of those." Zero showed his teeth in what wasn't quite a grin. "Let's get down to the first barricade and see what we surprise."

They'd gained other watchers on the crag edge and told them things in particular to look for in anything approaching, so there was no reason not to join the small groups holding the barricades. They made it to the lowest one, down at the High Road itself, before the riders came in sight.

Geoffrey strung his bow, but just waited. Even for a superb archer, they were at extreme range. The group at the Narrows looked to be about a dozen riders and the majority of them remained where they were for nearly an hour. They clearly hadn't been expecting resistance to their return.

Geoff thought at least two of them had ridden back, probably to carry word and get orders or reinforcements. That seemed confirmed by word passed by runners from the Great House. The runners also reported when another few riders were seen heading for the Narrows. Shortly after the young runners brought that news, they saw several mounted men arrive and join the likely enemies still waiting just at extreme arrow range. By then the old bartender, who was as it turned out the mayor as well, and two of her council had arrived near the barricade and walked the rest of the way down.

"I think Dyer's with them now," Geoff was saying as they arrived. "I think I recognize that hat. Bet you a new pair of riding boots I can hit him from here."

"You have been doing a good bit of walking," Zero agreed. "But could you kill him from here?"

"Not likely with these arrows, especially if he's Risen. Let's see if he'll come a little closer."

After observing the barricade for a bit longer, their likely enemies had something pale, perhaps a large white handkerchief, tied to a stick and waved vigorously at them. It was handed off to a rider who slowly walked his horse down the road toward the waiting defenders.

"If they don't know I'm with you, let's leave them find out later," said Geoff and adjusted his tartan blanket so it totally hid his pale hair and overhung his face.

"I do like the way ye think, Sir Geoffrey," remarked the mayor, who had finally introduced herself as Sarah Scott. "We've got a couple of the boys up on the crag, watching for anything trying to sneak around that way."

The approaching rider finally came within hailing distance. "Parley!" he shouted, waving the makeshift flag as though he had strong doubts it would be respected.

"We see ye," Sarah yelled back. "Come closer, man. I'm not going to screech back and forth at ye. Yer safe enough for now."

"You speak for the town?" he asked, riding closer.

"Ye'd know I do, if ye'd been paying any attention."

"I've come to ask for our men to be paroled. The Captain wants them released and he wants the Great House. In return, we'll leave you be."

"Like ye left us be in the main room of me own tavern? Well, lad, ye can tell yer Captain those men he left have been paroled to a better place. Stay and yer all quite welcome to join 'em. Or ye can ride north and take yer chances as wolfheads."

The rider blanched under his windburn. "All of them dead?"

"Dead," said Sarah. "And burned. Now, if ye've nothing more to say, be gone with ye!"

"You'll regret this, you old—"

Zero gestured and gave the man a sharp jerk by his scarf, cutting him off. "Manners, go-between. You wouldn't want to break your truce just now, would you? She wouldn't let me raise the others; but if you come back, she's said nothing about what I can do with you."

The man's eyes became huge in his red angry face and he paled again with equal suddenness as he met Zero's blue-purple stare. He abruptly yanked his horse around and spurred hard, sending it into a gallop back toward the rest of the raiders.

"I think that negotiation went well," Zero said, watching the rider flee.

"But now they know we have a necroknight with us," said one of the councilors.

"Yes. But they don't know how many. Or what else might be here." Zero's eyes glowed in the shadows under his hat. "Now we'll see what else they might send and if they truly are in cahoots with that resurrectionist."

"I'm wondering what Dyer wants with the keep," said Geoff.

"Stronghold," said Mayor Sarah. "Easy to retake Invercraig from the Great House. Once he'd get it, hard to pry him out again. And easy for him to set himself up as the new Laird."

"We heard him discussing it with his officers," said one of the councilors. "We're lucky he hadn't put more men into taking the place, but he sent most of them out into the dale looking for something."

"Lucky for us," said the second of the pair. "Probably not so much for others. And whatever he was looking for, did he find it?"

"Now that's not a happy thought. I'd guess no, or not all of it, since he still wants the Great House," said Zero, who was continuing to watch the raiders. "I'd suggest all the non-fighters get back up to the House, in case they try to make a charge on us."

Sarah and the councilors left with some of the message runners, taking the horses they'd ridden to the keep.

From what Zero and Geoff and the other defenders could see, the raiders had an even more elaborate discussion once their emissary had galloped back with Invercraig's message. And then, to everyone's surprise, the raiders all mounted their horses, turned around, and left through the Narrows.

"What?" said Zero, as the last of them vanished around the bend. "They never do that!"

"You just told them you're planning on raising their dead and sending them after their comrades," said one of the defenders, the town's blacksmith. "That Dyer bastard might be a nine-fathered spawn of demons, but he isn't stupid."

"She's right," said Geoffrey. "After what you and the townsfolk did, even if they don't know about us driving off the ghoul attack or the ones we've killed both in Invercraig and in the dale last night, the men have to be worried about just how many of us might be here. I wouldn't want to ride in here right now, with no more information than they've got."

"You've got the best eyes between the pair of us, Geoff. Run up and see if you can tell which way they're headed," Zero suggested.

"And Tom, lad, you run quick to the overlook and see if there's anyone on the Craigburn Path," the blacksmith ordered one of the boys who was with them. "Beat it back here if you see anyone coming."

"Overlook?" asked Zero

"There's a squirrel's own trail from the far edge of the cemetery up to a rock above the burn. You can see a mile or more of the path from there. Admittedly, not all in one clear line, but if anyone's moving along it, you've got some warning before they get close."

If he hadn't been in semi-charge of protecting the road, Zero would have gone with the boy. He hated being the one who had to wait, but that's where circumstance had put him.

***

Geoffrey came back first, finally trotting down the path to announce, "They picked up a few more near the MacKintoshes' steading and just kept riding north."

"I guess there's a first time for everything," said Zero.

"Do you think we can go back to our homes now?" asked Estrid the blacksmith after her boy Tom finally got back; just before Zero had been about to leave to check on him. Tom had seen nothing other than birds moving on the Craigburn path.

"I don't know," Zero told her, looking out toward the Narrows. "There were ghouls out in the dale last night and there's at least one resurrectionist still unaccounted for. I'd recommend we wait and make sure this isn't a ruse." It was a thought he found himself repeating several times before he was able to reach the mayor and her councilors.

Despite some grumbling, no one was anxious to risk another attack by ghouls or worse. Plans were made and scouting parties organized. Zero was able to secure the chestnut gelding he'd been riding and a big bay mare for Geoffrey. Broken Sky showed no interest in joining them, seemly content to continue recovering from helping to revive and restrain Geoff from the night before.

Geoff said, "We've packed a lot into just a couple of days. Do we ever slow down?"

Zero shook his head. "We'll slow down when we're dead. Again."

"Heh. I suppose."

Zero didn't want Geoffrey going into combat without being nearby to support him. Otherwise he would have sent his squire with one of the other scouting groups. Instead they wished the others luck and headed out toward the dale, turning toward where the old military road was said to cross the far end. Somewhere along that ancient road, Merryweather Steward had seen Dyer meeting with the necromancer they sought.

Blackthorn was coming into bloom in patches. Zero still wore the dryads' favors as did his chestnut. Even the flowers he'd shared with Geoffrey were still as fresh as if they'd just been picked, blackthorn and the rowan out of season. Zero had a light hunting bow, a couple of hunting broadheads and one of the blackthorn arrows he'd been given. Geoffrey had the rest of the dryad's gift, minus the two he'd used, and a pair of war arrows, punch points which could penetrate mail and cheap plate. They kept the horses at a trot, but occasionally pulled up to let Zero send his seeking tendrils of arcane energy probing through deep brush and small patches of woodland.

They'd left the whitewashed farmhouses and cots behind them as they drew closer to the military road. Sunlight made the day a pleasant ride, but the scent of blackthorn was a reminder of their purpose.

They finally found a necromancer in one of the copses, a stand of hawthorn and ancient yew around the edges of a stonewalled cemetery just off the military road.

New ghouls who could have been mistaken for living men but for their purple glowing eyes mingled with fleshless skeletons held together only by the necromancer's darkly glimmering magick among the stubs of gravestones. The smell of worms and fresh-turned earth was heavy in the air and the pair of necroknights' mortal horses broke into a sweat. They danced and stomped and refused to go further.

"Have you come to join me?"

The voice was clear, but felt more than heard. Geoffrey shuddered and Zero flinched at that touch, entirely too like the mocking voice of the Risen Tsar he'd once been forced to obey. Whether this was the second necromancer they had seen at the MacIver farm wasn't clear, but they hadn't heard that one speak. *Surely*, they shared glances and the unspoken thought, *there can't be more than two resurrectionists wandering about in the same area at the same time, can there?*

"Not by those expressions, I'd say. No? I could give you such better mounts."

The horses, as though they understood, had started backing up.

"Well, if you won't serve willingly, I'm not going to force you. I've *seen* how well that worked for Ivan. If you're here, I don't suppose my bloodkin took that little town back? Or the Great House above it? No to that as well?" There was an impression of a sigh of annoyance.

"Well, go then. Go. Shoo! You want to be free? Stay free. But stay out of my way. I have things to do at that House and they are no concern of yours."

"There you would be wrong," said Zero, wondering if the speaker had a way to actually hear him. "I had enough of your kind in the Russ."

"Oh, to the Nine Spiraling Hells with you!" growled the necromancer, who had, it seemed, heard him. "A hero and his brainless squire. Well, if you won't leave of your own volition, perhaps you will with proper incentive. Should have brought warmounts, little necroknights." The voice ceased.

The ghouls and skeletons charged.

Lazy Lob and the bay mare, likely wiser than their riders, spun and bolted. Geoffrey and Zero hung on and let them run.

"Well, we found out where they are," said Geoffrey as his bay caught up with Zero's tiring and raggedly-breathing chestnut after the horses' first mad sprint.

"Yes," said Zero. "And now we're leading them back to Invercraig. Your girl's got more endurance than this boy does, keep going. Warn them of what's coming. And don't waste your lightnings."

"Zero!"

"I'll get there if I can. I made a promise to the children. I'm not going to throw myself away without trying hard to keep that promise."

"Damnit!" Geoffrey looked as though he wanted to disobey, but he clucked to his mare and she pulled ahead of the faltering chestnut.

Slowly she pulled away and Zero eased the gelding back down to a walk, swung down, and began leading

Lob along their retreat. They had a good start on the ghouls and skeletons, but even normal humans could eventually run down a horse.

Zero started looking for a spot to make a stand if they caught up. He thought it was more than likely to be when they caught up, not if. To pass the time, he sang softly to the weary, wheezing gelding,

"Green grows the holly.
So doth the ivy.
Though winter blasts blow e'er so high
Green grows the holly.

"Green grows the holly.
So doth the rowan.
Though Scots pines grow e'er so high
Green grows the holly.

"Green grows the holly
So doth the yew tree.
Though the pyres glow e'er so high
Green grows the holly."

They came to a lochan near where the remains of stone walls suggested a farm or at least a pasture had once been. Zero and Lob both drank, but Zero pulled the horse away before he could make himself sick with the cold water from the pond. The ghouls were closer, Geoffrey and his bay a dot almost lost in the folds of the dale. And beyond them, Zero could see parts of the coastal road and the glint of the sea channel far in the distance.

He kept walking. The shadows grew longer. The ghouls seemed to gather strength from the coming darkness. They were close now, close enough he could make out individuals running in the pack. Lob was growing anxious at their nearness.

"Shall we make them work a little harder for their meat?" Zero asked the chestnut and jumped high to catch the saddle and scramble on.

A howl rose up from the ghouls and Lob tried to bolt again, but Zero held him down to a hand gallop, a little faster than a canter and eventually got him back to a trot. He'd gained distance on the ghouls again, but he could feel it wasn't going to last. They just made the coastal road, but they'd not make the Narrows, given the way the chestnut had again started coughing and wheezing.

"Well, fuck," said Zero. "A wind-broken horse. This is why necroknights don't ride normal living horses. I did this to you, didn't I, old fellow?"

He pulled Lob up and swung down one last time. "I'll not run you to death just to save myself, Lazy Lob."

Zero knotted the reins so they wouldn't fall under the gelding's feet and yank his mouth or trip him. "But you do need to get away from me, old man."

Zero slapped the horse hard on the rump, putting a touch of his own darkness behind it. Lob spooked and bucked, coughed again, and began trotting toward Invercraig. "At least he isn't stopping to graze," Zero observed to nothing in particular. "I hope he smells the other horses and keeps on going."

Zero turned to check on the location of the ghouls. They'd made up a lot of the distance between themselves and Zero in the brief time since he'd dismounted. Seeing him looking at them, the ghouls howled again and put on a burst of speed of their own.

"Come on, then, you bastards!" Zero taunted, blue ice glittering in the waning sunlight where it struck his frosted sword and the blackthorn club.

Behind him there was a clatter of hooves on the hard road. A blast of freezing air gusted over him, cold, but not enough to do harm. "Bugger you!" Zero pivoted, thinking the necromancer had somehow used the Hidden Ways to get behind him.

Instead, his warmount Bessariel had finally arrived. She circled him, dropping down to her knees beside him so he could mount. He leapt astride, feeling a surge of hope. And hoped the saddle wasn't loose and likely to dump him back onto the road right in front of the ghouls.

Bessariel rose to her feet. Rose and leaped, up and forward, rear hooves hitting something behind them with a meaty smack. Then they were running for the coastal road and the Narrows, two hoarfrost-covered armored knights flanking them at the gallop, screaming ghouls chasing madly after. Zero turned and almost struck at the nearest knight before recognizing they were friends.

"Hrothgar! Bennett!"

"Zero! You madman! Almost killed over a horse. Again!"

"You could see me from the Hidden Ways? Well, you know me, Bennett! And the odds didn't look good for us making it much further."

"We could see you from the coast road," yelled Bennett. "Bess pulled us along into the Ways with her when she went to rescue you."

The small group caught up with Lob and herded the exhausted gelding before them, all making the hard turn through the hastily opened barricade at the entrance to the road to the Great House. Zero and the human knights pulled up to wheel back on the undead behind them, while Lob immediately dropped to a sweating, wheezing shuffle.

Zero glimpsed the blacksmith's boy, Tom, grab Lob's reins and keep the weary, wheezing gelding moving up the castle road. Then the ghouls arrived.

Ghouls were usually smarter fighters, but this lot had almost caught up with Zero just one time too many to be able to think rationally. They threw themselves at the barricade in their desire to get to him, snapping, clawing, and trying to pull it and its defenders to pieces. A flurry of rocks pitched down from the switchback above helped break the ghouls' mad charge, but by the sheer force of their outrage, some made it through, running up and over their companions and jumping into the humans on the other side.

The pikes and bills of the ground-bound defenders kept most of the mob at distance. Behind them, the Caliburn war horses fought as extensions of their riders. Bessariel and Zero fought like a pair of warriors long used to attacking together and defending one another, intercepting the ghouls among the pike-wielders or the ones trying to hamstring the knights' horses. With their aid, the villagers held against the first attack.

The smarter ghouls stopped charging and withdrew out of easy bow range, dragging their own dead or crippled comrades. Out of range of rocks and most arrows, the ghouls fell upon those dead, tearing them to pieces and eating them. Some shared bits with those too damaged to walk until they'd eaten enough to partially heal and could stand again on their own. The defenders looked on from behind the remains of their barricade, horrified and in some cases, violently emptying their own stomachs' contents. Then they retreated to the next barricade while the ghouls were busy.

"Get anyone bitten up to Goody Greneglais to have those wounds cleaned out," yelled Zero and Estrid the blacksmith at the same time. "Send down replacements,"

Estrid added. Zero shouted, “Have your vicar purify the wounds too!”

They looked at each other and laughed, Estrid with a touch of hysteria.

“Easy. You’re doing great.” Zero looked around at the other defenders. “You’re all doing great. I’ve fought beside regulars who broke in the face of ghoul charges.”

“Becoming a sergeant, are you, Zero?” asked the slighter built of the knights.

“Don’t wish that on me, Bennett! But Morrigan’s smile, it’s good to see you again. And Hrothgar too!”

The Dane looked up where he’d dismounted and was checking the legs of his dark brown war horse and said gravely, “Good to see you still on this side of the Rainbow Bridge, Zerollen diGriz.”

The three exchanged warriors’ grasps. Zero said, “I was hoping Bessariel’d wait for someone to follow her back, but I can’t believe you chased her all the way here from Thornhill.”

“We knew you’d gotten yourself into something when she came storming in.” Bennett looked around, taking in the hastily engineered defenses, and the townfolk rushing to bring water and food to the defenders during the lull in the fighting. “This is a bit much, even for you.”

“What’s out there?” asked Hrothgar, ever practical.

“Currently, we got a resurrectionist – a necromancer - who wants something in the Great House. It’s raised ghouls, which you’ve seen, but there’s also a scary number of skeletons coming this way. Maybe zombies as well, but I hadn’t seen any of those.”

“Powerful?”

“It was talking to me in my head. But it seemed more interested in chasing Geoffrey and I off than fighting us directly. So,” Zero shrugged. “I’m not sure quite what we're dealing with, but it's powerful enough things will be messy."

"Messy enough you finally took a squire?" asked Bennett.

"I had him before we knew there was a resurrectionist around. Geoff was an accident," Zero admitted.

"Accident?"

"He was already tainted. I'm still surprised he hadn't risen before I found him, but being face down in a spring might have been slowing him from manifesting."

"You have all the luck, Zerollen."

"They're back!" someone yelled from the barricade and they returned to the fight.

The ghouls had begun regrouping, but an arrow from somewhere higher up the road flashed into their midst and through the eye socket of the one giving commands. That would-be leader fell, disrupting the ghouls' organization once again. This time the ghouls grabbed their fallen officer and retreated further onto the beach.

"Looks like they're settling in for a siege," warned Bennett, who was still mounted and peering around at the feeding ghouls and the remains of the first barricade. "Or waiting for full night to fall. Whoever's taking command down there is having them pull even further back toward that narrow squeeze through the rocks on the edge of the beach. You said there are more coming?"

"Sadly enough, yes. A lot of skeletons. Maybe some zombies. Possibly more ghouls. And the resurrectionist talked like it's been around since the first Rising."

Hrothgar cursed inventively. Bennett frowned and nodded.

Geoffrey came warily down from the bailey, bow held with an arrow to hand for a quick draw, with several of Invercraig's women and older girls following in what armor and with what weapons they'd scavenged from the dead raiders. Behind them, Hector came along with several other children carrying buckets of water for defenders and horses alike.

The boy surprised everyone once he'd set down his buckets by sprinting over to Zero and wrapping his arms around the necroknight. "I thought you'd not make it back," he said, muffled into Zero's breastplate.

"Easy, lad. I'm still here, but I'm not that safe to touch right now," Zerollen said, gently removing the child. "I'm still here," he repeated to Geoffrey who seemed both surprised by Hector's actions and as though he were considering joining him in hugging Zero.

Hector sighed and stepped back, shivering a bit and rubbing furtively at his eyes. Bessariel chose that moment to step up and nose the boy, wuffling at his hair with interest. Hector squirmed away, turning to look at her.

"That's your warmount? She's beautiful!"

"That she is," Geoffrey agreed.

Bessariel arched her neck and practically preened at the compliment, then nosed Zerollen considerably harder than she had the boy.

"Yes, my lady," Zero said with good humor, reaching up to scratch behind one of her ears. "I'll see to that girth in a moment." He looked over at Geoffrey and the two Caliburn knights. "Your horses could use some rest after that sprint and skirmish.

"Always thinking of the horses first. But I see you've been collecting companions. Whoever are these two?" asked Bennett, tone half amused, half approving.

"This," said Zero, gesturing to the boy, "Is Hector MacLean. He and his sisters were the original reason for my delaying here. And this is Sir Geoffrey Hartsbane, my squire."

Before continuing, Zero gave Bennett a questioning look. The slender knight shrugged in answer.

"Geoff, Hector, may I introduce the Lady Sir Bennetta Benoit and Sir Hrothgar of the Dane March, knights of the Order of Caliburn and old battle comrades of mine."

Geoff made a leg, while Hector did something between a more old-fashioned bob and an elven bow from the waist. Zero didn't think the boy's eyes could get much bigger, especially when Sir Bennetta glared and snapped, "Call me Bennett!"

Hrothgar glanced up from where he'd just pulled Dragonbiter away from stuffing his head into another bucket. He frowned slightly under his long, thick mustache. He gave a polite bow of acknowledgement, but his attention was more on the Great House road and the location of the enemy.

"Not really a road for lance charges," he observed.

"Not until this last turn, but worse moreso for anyone trying to get up here," said Zero, familiar with the Dane's suspicious nature.

"What do they have for stables, though?"

"The stables seemed in decent shape, what I saw of them last night. No one was trying to break into them when the Great House was originally attacked. At least, not until after the house fell." Zero grimaced at the thought, one he would have preferred to leave forgotten. He studied the ghouls, the few still in sight, and decided he agreed with Bennett on their current plans, "Come, I'll show you where they are."

***

Broken Sky greeted them with an excited whinny as they crested onto the flat which was the old upper baily. He was particularly interested in Bessariel. He arched his neck and trotted up and down the fence line with his tail flagged. Bess left Zero and trotted over to inspect him.

They met, sniffing noses and squealing at each other more like two stallions than stallion and mare. After striking and posturing at each other, Bessariel spun and gave a warning kick. Broken Sky took several steps back, but lifted his upper lip in something between his laugh and an 'oh-you-smell-good' stallion flirt.

Zero grinned and shook his head, then showed Bennett and Hrothgar where to stable their horses. Hector offered to help give them a rubdown. Zero pulled off Bessariel's tack, but otherwise left her and Broken Sky to flirt. He found another child was watching over the animals who he was able to send to get some warm food for his friends.

It turned out, as he'd expected from how long it had taken them to arrive, they'd spent little time in the Hidden Ways. They'd only gotten pulled into them by Bessariel in the last parts of their trip as she became more anxious to reach her rider. Hellebore and Dragonbiter, respectively Bennett's and Hrothgar's war horses, had followed willingly enough, having fought alongside the black warmount often during the northern campaigns against the Risen. Zero was pleased to see Lob had been given a spot in the stable as well as a blanket, even if it was motheaten and ragged. The chestnut was dozing with his head almost brushing the straw.

They'd gotten the Caliburn knights' horses bedded comfortably enough by the time the stablegirl came back to tell them food was waiting for them in the great hall. It was good to grab a mug of heated and spiced ale with Geoffrey while the others quickly washed off the road dust and ate. The warmth of the hall was pleasant, even lurking near the doors as the two necroknights did. Zero was calmer, no longer unconsciously pulling warmth from everything around himself.

He knew it wouldn't last.

In fact, he'd barely had time to introduce the pair of Caliburn Knights to Mayor Sarah and the other leaders of the human defenders when one of the villagers ran in and interrupted, "There's an army coming from the dale!"

Everyone ran out to the overlook where they could see into the dale. In the last of the day's light, they could see movement. It was not quite an army, but certainly enough beings to give the small group of defenders a serious reason to worry.

"Looks like mostly those things we saw, with ghouls acting as sergeants or officers," Geoffrey said softly to Zero.

"Did you see the resurrectionist?"

"No."

"With that many of the mindless, it's going to have to be closer this time."

"Good," said Hrothgar from Zero's other side. "Maybe we'll get to strike directly at it. That would solve much trouble."

"It would, but it's strong. It won't be easy if we have to fight it."

Hrothgar gave Zero an appraising look.

"Not *that* strong." Zero shook his head. "At least, I don't think so, but enough to be a problem once it gets mad at us."

Healer Greneglais was coming out of the House when they came back from the overlook. She had left off her skirt and was dressed in a leather coat rather like a long gambeson over high drover-styled boots. And her bright hair was uncovered and loose under a leather cap styled like a swooping hawk. In the torch-lit gloaming, she was fey and beautiful. And with her, she carried the softly glowing staff from her hospice's sign.

Everyone stopped and stared at her in shock. There was no denying the Seelie blood somewhere in her family now.

"Goody Greneglais!" began Mayor Sarah. "Bridget, what -?"

"I've done all I can for the children and the wounded for now," Healer Greneglais said. "Now is time I turned to my other skills, if we are to save the children from the fever which grips them."

She turned to Zero and the other knights. "I'm not a warmage, but I can put light where you will best need it."

"Excellent," said Bennett. "Come, lady, let's us be starting." She led Healer Greneglais back toward the overlook. Both were already deep in discussion of where magelight might be used to the best effect.

"Why are they going that way?" asked one of Mayor Sarah's councilors.

"Skeletons climb," said Hrothgar shortly.

"Everything but dressed stone," Geoffrey added, looking vaguely ill. He sounded like he'd seen them do just that at least once during his time as a soldier.

Zero asked, "Mayor Sarah, would you assign Sir Bennett and Healer Greneglais at least one runner to carry messages if they find anything trying to come at us from up the cliffs or down the mountain?"

"I'll see to that, Sir Zerollen. You and these other good knights should have messenger runners as well."

"That would be appreciated, milady." Zerollen gave her a deep elven bow.

"Don't be a saucy Jack with me, lad," the old bartender scolded.

Zero looked up, but kept his bow. "Goodwoman Mayor Sarah, I meant only the deepest respect. You will always be worthy of the title 'Lady' in my eyes."

The old woman smiled and colored a bit more than the torchlight accounted for. "Stand up, lad, and get about your business then."

Zero straightened up from his bow and did just that. "Tell the defenders to have rocks ready to roll or drop on anything trying to come up the road or the cliffs," he told them before heading back toward the house road.

9: THE BATTLE FOR CRAIG HOUSE

"If the ghouls weren't already here, I'd hold them at the Narrows," Bennett commented, echoing Zero's thoughts of the previous day.

"Until they came over the rock," Hrothgar replied, running a sharpening stone over the edge of his axe.

"Yes, but the necromancer will have to be closer to give them accurate commands to get them climbing over the rock."

"And this will be good for us how?" asked one of the villagers.

"If we can lure the resurrectionist out, then we can find a way to kill it. Kill it and the mindless will stop or be easier to take control of," said Zero. "If I can do that, they'll be easier to give a final death. And we'll be rid of the resurrectionist and any more undead it might be making."

"Somehow, I don't think that's going to be as simply done as it sounds," said the villager, peering down the High Road toward the stone outcroppings of the Narrows, which were becoming only dark shapes against the last of the gloaming light.

"I don't think so either," agreed Geoffrey.

Zero nodded, watching shadows moving on the High Road. "Nothing that involves us ever is. Shh, bide a moment."

The others fell silent, as did the villagers among them.

Zero tilted his head, listening. Faintly, he heard scratch, scratch, scratch, in a marching cadence, getting louder. “Light the road.”

Geoffrey thrust a fishing arrow wrapped with oiled linen into an open lantern until it caught, then launched it out into the verge of plants between the road and the beach. The scratching sounds picked up speed. Healer Greneglais took the burning arrow as her mark and summoned light, brightening an area much larger than the small glow which had lit her sign. She laid down two more patches of light, just barely overlapping an edge of the first and then the second, before Bennett hurried her away. Startled ghouls spooked out of the light, but most of the leading group of skeletons continued marching onward toward the road up to the Great House.

Some rocks pelted down among them, doing minor damage.

Hrothgar bellowed, “Kill the skeletons, not the road!” just before one of the ghouls yelled “Charge the ramp! Kill the living!” and the madness began.

“Where did the necromancer possibly find all of these?” complained Hrothgar. “Don’t you people bless your dead?”

“Old battlefields off the military road?” Zero suggested. “Unconsecrated graveyards?”

The defenders’ axes, maces, and hammers sent chunks of bone flying everywhere. The blackthorn club with the dark dryad’s blessing was particularly devastating to the skeletons and it seemed to gain blooms for every undead Zero struck down. Indeed, both necroknights fought in a perfume of blackthorn and rowan, and even though mindless, the skeletons moved away from them when they had room. This put more pressure on their companions, but it left the pair freer to strike the undead bones down.

But still, the skeletons just kept coming. They carried weapons of their own, even if some of them were nothing more than rusty hilts and scraps of broken shields. Each had to have its head struck off or smashed. Otherwise, whatever remained of the body would try to drag itself back into the fight.

Despite their best efforts, the living defenders were taking wounds. In the flickering shadows between torches, strikes and dodges were misjudged in the deepening darkness. Goodwoman Greneglais' light spells were limited, not only in size, but in how many she could create. Some had to be held in reserve for the expected attack up the cliffs. So, while the defenders could clearly see the ranks pushing forward and the rocks being flung down on them, sometimes to good effect, they fought in shadow. Blood and broken bones made the footing increasingly treacherous. And their weapon arms were growing tired, while the undead stepped over broken, motionless skeletons and kept swinging at them.

Then the warning they'd all been expecting came. Skeletons were beginning to climb the cliffs. And ghouls were loosing flights of arrows into the rock-throwing defenders on the cliff top. Just as that news came, a group of ghouls stepped into the light at the edge of the road and released a flight over the barricade. At close to point blank range, most of them struck targets. Some clattered harmlessly, but others fell through gaps in armor or found uncovered flesh. Others punched straight through the cobbled-together armor taken from Dyer's raiders. Shrieks rose from the defenders and several went down.

The ghouls redrew and loosed another flight into the fight on the Great House road. Defenders fell and several more were wounded. The skeletons pressed forward, crowding into gaps in the line, leaving off striking to pull at the barricade.

"Back!" roared Estrid. "Retreat to the switchback!"

"Get our people up and out of here," yelled Geoffrey, stepping over a fallen defender to sweep the area before him with axe and mace. Zero matched him, using the undead's aversion to the fae-blessed rowan sunwheel cross and the blackthorn club to force back more than just his reach accounted for. Behind them, the villagers grabbed their dead and wounded and retreated.

Seeing their prey retreat, the ghouls howled and jeered, and loosed yet another flight into the group with predictable results. The skeletons rallied and threw themselves forward at the two necroknights.

"Hrothgar! Get the humans back. Geoffrey and I will hold them. Go!"

"With all your powers?" asked Hrothgar, guessing at what was coming.

"Hells, yes. Move them. Now!"

"What are we doing?" asked Geoffrey.

"This," said Zero. And he deliberately released the control he kept over his necroknight's ability to draw in warmth from everything around him. Hoarfrost immediately began forming over his weapons, except for where the blackthorn and rowan blooms remained defiant. Frost spread outward, coating the road, the skeletons, and the cliff edges. Humans behind him yelped and hurried away faster. Skeletons scrabbled to follow and slipped instead, the blackthorn club flashing down to shatter a skull as easily as if it were an egg. Zero swung it back up, taking out another skeleton's sword arm.

Zero kicked another back, overbalancing several, and tucked his sword momentarily under his arm to reach out and touch Geoffrey, removing the last controls he held over his squire's abilities. He heard Geoff gasp in surprise, and then they were both swinging into skeletons.

Zero almost fumbled his sword in reclaiming it, but soon both club and sword were leaving a fine trail of frost and white blossoms through the damp sea air. Beside him, Geoffrey's strikes left a dark miasma over those he hit, rot attacking the bones and disrupting the animating force keeping them together and moving. Bones cracked and shattered or fell apart, but still more skeletons pushed forward. Even more dangerous to the necroknights and the other defenders were the war arrows from the ghoul archers, designed to punch through mail and plate, fired by archers' whose bow arms never grew tired. Geoffrey's own marksmanship had shown those slender missiles could quite effectively slay the undead. Though the two held the road, the sheer unrelenting assault pushed them back slowly.

While Geoffrey set himself almost into the stone with each careful step back, Zero glided with frightening ease over the frost-slicked cobbles, only to brace himself into them with each strike. But the necromancer, wherever it hid, kept throwing its skeletal minions at them with no regard to the creatures' durability or lack thereof. Even necroknights could be worn down with so little life and arcane energy to feed on.

"There's still more," came a yell from above. "Let them have some of the damned road, Zero!"

In unspoken accord, both Zero and Geoffrey sent an attack of flesh-freezing wind and wicked violet lightning through the skeletons and into the ghoul archers, wounding many and causing some of the bowstrings to break. Then they turned and ran, leaping or dodging boulders rolled down the road at their pursuers. Geoffrey slipped on a patch of bloody stones and almost fell, but managed catching himself on his hands, and scrabbling along until he could get his feet under him again. “How close dare we get to the others?” he yelled to Zero.

“We’re close enough. Hold!” Zero warned, hopping over a boulder to get next to his squire and steady him.

“How do I—”

“Like this.” Zero braced the two of them, hoping no mis-rolled rock or eager skeleton closed with them for the time he needed. The flush of battle actually made the connection between them stronger. “Feel me pushing at your magick? Pull it back. That’s it. Like that. Yes.”

His own need for warmth made controlling his special ability more difficult, but he pulled it in until he was at least no longer moving in a cloud of tiny snow crystals. Running again, they made it to the next barricade with enough lead on their pursuers they were able to slip through a daringly opened gap.

They retreated to the back of the group, trying to stay close enough to help, but not so near as to provoke their hunger more than it already was. Someone brought them hot, steaming water and that eased a little of the pain as it warmed them internally. Zero pulled out the little jar of green paste and offered it to Geoffrey. He sniffed at it cautiously before letting Zero test it on one of his wounds. Though it caused him pain, this time he was more tolerant of the healing it did than Zero. It took the whole contents of the pot to close their injuries and force arrow heads back out of their bodies. Nothing could really be done for their tattered armor beyond swapping out some pieces for bits pulled off the injured or dead.

All too soon, Zero and Geoff were back on the line, relieving tiring or wounded villagers. At least the remaining ghoul archers couldn't launch volleys with the same effectiveness, not without coming into a downpour of rocks and other missiles hurled from further up the cliff. But between their volleys and the climbing skeletons, rock tosses at the archers below were becoming fewer rapidly as the surviving clifftop defenders turned their attentions to dropping stones down the cliff at the climbers.

"Can you do that again? Your magick attacks?" asked Estrid of the pair. "If we don't fall back soon, we risk getting cut off from the inner bailey.

Geoffrey looked to Zero, who nodded.

"This will be the last," Zero warned. "Pull back all the way to the upper bailey. It sounds like they need you up there. And we won't be safe to be near…." His voice trailed off as he considered possibilities. "Tell Hrothgar and Bennett."

The defenders retreated a few at a time. They moved further up the road, sending wounded behind the wood and stone wall which had been thrown up to block access to the outer bailey. But despite Zero's suggestion, not all of them took shelter. Some remained to fling stones down into the skeletons.

Zero and Geoffrey were covering more and more of the line. The skeletons bunched and forced forward harder. If the necroknights didn't do something more drastic soon, they would have the enemy breaking through.

"Light them up now?" suggested one of the humans still with them. "Like you did with the ice and lightning?"

"We'd likely kill you, if we did," Zerollen warned. He swung the blackthorn club and smashed a boney arm tugging on part of the barricade.

"Better you than getting torn apart by those things," the old fisherman said. "Still, I'd rather die at sea than here. If we run now, can you do it?"

Geoff already had flickers of red lightning gleaming violet across the arcane blue glow of his eyes. "Run!" he said forcefully as the skeletons threw themselves into the barricade again.

"Run or die here!" Zero yelled in agreement, directing the words as much toward the undead facing them as the humans still at their sides.

The humans ran. The skeletons milled for just a moment as though their controller had heard the necroknight's threat.

It was enough.

With a ripping sound and the shattering of bones, lightning tore through a cloud of fine, fast moving ice pellets. A chunk of bone tore into Zero's cheek and lodged against his teeth, but he was too busy taking advantage of the skeletons' momentary confusion to bother with it. Sword and blackthorn beat the skeletons back, as did Geoffrey's mace and axe. Skeletons slipped and fell in the sudden ice and snow underfoot.

But others clambered over them.

This time the retreat was run a few steps or do a quick back up, with skeletons crowding them hard, trying to slip past to pull down the retreating humans. Ghouls followed, even when another blast of lightnings and icy, snow-filled wind scythed through them. Then Geoff did something which sent a cloud of blackness rolling across the enemy, leaving their bones and some of their weapons pitted and shearing flesh and muscle off the ghouls. The stones and rocks thrown by the defenders further up were more effective in snapping pitted bones and more of the skeletons fell.

The ghouls howled and charged again.

Zero pulled all of the damp remaining in the nearby air and some of the already fallen snow and ice and turned it into a frozen mass over and through what remained of the barricade before sprinting up and around the last switchback with frost flowing over the road at every step. Geoff was at his side in a fog of black specks like hungry midges.

Rocks fell among the skeletons who managed to pursue them, knocking some over the low curb and back down onto the road below. Ghouls loosed arrows at the stone throwers and other defenders, only to be forced back by the two necroknights' magicks. Finally, all of the humans were behind the hastily built wall protecting the upper bailey with only Zero and Geoff still on the road.

Zombies were starting to appear in the enemy ranks, likely raised from fallen ghouls who hadn't been eaten by their comrades. They were tougher to drop, since most had armor and weapons, but there were fewer archers among them than there had been, and their arrows were dangerous only by mischance. The handful of ghoul archers were still a problem however. The necroknights and the living defenders concentrated on them whenever they had the opportunity.

Zero and Geoff took a spot down from the upper bailey wall and held there. No one living dared come to their aid as the very air around them was now deadly with Geoff's midges and Zero's whirling shards of ice. And from what the two could hear, the battle on top of the cliff in the upper bailey was still going on.

They noted, however, some of the ghouls facing them would occasionally break and retreat, some going so far as to go over the road edge to avoid passing through those still attacking.

"What the hell is that about?" asked Geoff, flinging lightnings and his black midges into another group of skeletons who'd come too close.

"The resurrectionist is likely fighting on too many fronts. His control is breaking over the ones who can still think for themselves. It was a fight like this against the Caliburn Knights and the Chorus of Steel in the Russ which broke Ivan's control over the company I belonged to - though we were facing Sir Tercel and the Newgate twins then. But I think I wasn't nearly this hungry at the time."

"Don't talk about being hungry. I might rip into the next ghoul to gets near me. And I think I'm actually tired."

"No more lightning."

"Says the man who is only standing because he's freezing his feet to the ground."

Bessariel daringly joined them then, her metal-shod hooves and wicked teeth smashing skeletons to bits. Her presence beside them gave the battered pair some respite, and Zero's bond with her shielded the war mare from his and Geoffrey's magicks. But still the skeletons came.

***

Until, finally, sometime in the wee hours, there were no more skeletons.

Instead, a rider came up the icy, bone- and gore-spattered road. A few zombies rose from bodies which had been ghouls and followed, but they were very few. Still, any at all were extra foes the defenders would be hard pressed to hold off, even without the necromancer being with them.

As the necromancer appeared on the edge of the outer bailey, it was suddenly lit by one of Goody Greneglais' lights, giving Zero, Geoffrey and the living defenders their first look at the enemy. But even the necroknights and Zero's warmount were too tired to do more than hold their ground as it looked around at the carnage and nodded. Whether the fae-blessed blackthorn club and the sunwheel cross of rowan twigs affected it was hard to tell, but it didn't come closer. To Zero and Geoff's horror, it didn't look like the one who had passed the MacIver farm.

"It's you two again," it said, and they at least had the relief of recognizing the voice as the one who had chased them from Craigsdale and not an until-now-un-encountered necromancer. "Still together, surprisingly enough. I gave you the opportunity to leave. And yet, here you are. I see you found at least one warmount along the way."

Bessariel showed the necromancer her very unhorselike fangs, but remained at Zero's side.

The necromancer shook its head. "I can wait a little longer. I'll even let you give your dead to the pyre and not raise them." It shrugged. "You won't stay here forever." It turned its mount to leave.

"No, they likely won't stay," said another voice. "But I will. And you will not threaten my people again."

Startled, the necromancer jerked around toward the spectral laird who had manifested right behind him.

The laird screamed in good imitation of a banshee's wail directly at both rider and mount. The sound dropped the few living defenders outside the House to their knees and staggered Zero and Geoff. The horselike creature the necromancer rode disincorporated under the torrent of sound, leaving its rider sprawled in a horse-sized pile of stinking slime and bones.

The necromancer rolled over, spitting out a mouthful of goop. “Oh, you’re going to pay for that, old man,” it said, this time in a completely different voice than before.

“How many of you are in there?” Zero managed to ask.

The laird looked taken aback at this response to his attack. “Dunstan?” he asked incredulously.

“Don’t talk to it,” warned Zero.

At the same time, still in that other voice, the necromancer said, “Hello, Father. You’re not looking well these days.”

“Better than you, it would seem,” observed the old laird. “That’s not the body I remember you being born to.”

“Unlike you, I choose my servants for more than aesthetic reasons.”

“Touche’,” his spectral father conceded.

Meanwhile, purple-red and purple-black energies flowed just on the edge of vision around the two as they fenced with more than words.

Zero and Geoff exchanged glances.

Stay! Zero mouthed.

Geoff shook his head minutely in denial. He nodded toward the zombies.

Zero started to object and Bessariel stepped between them. She turned her head and lipped Zero’s shoulder, her fangs clicking against what was left of his armor there.

“All right, my lady,” he whispered in acceptance. “Both of you be careful.”

Out of the corner of his eye, Zero could see flashes between the spectral laird and the necromancer growing brighter as they continued to exchange insults and family history with increasing virulence. Beyond those two feuding entities, Bennett and Healer Greneglais were herding the wounded and the gawkers from the Great House back inside. Hrothgar was helping Estrid with the few defenders still holding.

He caught himself licking his lips as he noted how ragged those defenders appeared. *Don't*, he warned himself as the predator within him started to focus on them. Or perhaps he caught a warning from Bessariel, he felt certainly weary enough to hear actual words from her as easily as if she spoke to him.

He started circling around the fight, moving in sudden rushes and pauses and painfully slow shifting of his weight from one foot to another, trying to avoid the necromancer noticing his changing position. The purply-blackness had intensified around the necromancer and the laird. Neither were sniping verbally at one another now, both faces mirrored grim concentration instead. But Zero had seen necromancers playing with their prey and wasn't reassured. He could also see trails of purple light leading from the necromancer to the zombies, though the smooth flows of that energy were becoming more erratic. The energy seemed to be flowing — when it did flow — more toward the necromancer than to the zombies it was controlling.

That would be due to whatever Geoffrey and Bessariel are doing to the zombies, Zero thought.

Then the purple trails feeding energy into the necromancer grew to the size and solidity of a ship's hawsers. There was a sudden sickly yellow-green glow flaring over the spectral laird, taking on the appearance of manacles and leg irons binding the old warrior. The specter remained visible, but collapsed partially into the stone of the bailey.

"Who is master now, old man?" panted the necromancer in its own voice, before Dunstan overrode it with his own pleased chuckle. And then the dually-possessed body turned with such frightening swiftness to confront Zero, the necroknight could hear the possessed necromancer's joints popping, "I haven't forgotten *you*! *Free Undead!*" Dunstan sneered through the body he was possessing. "What a joke that is. You are only free until a master reclaims you."

There was pressure and light and pain inside Zero's mind, like the worst of dazzle headaches, the ultimate hangover, a mace to the head. This necromancer wasn't even there in his own flesh and was still far stronger than Zero had expected.

Zero found himself on his hands and knees, uncertain how he'd gotten there.

Oh, Gods! What have I done this time? he asked himself, unsure how much time might have passed. Years had passed the last time he'd been subjugated and bound to another's will.

But the spectral laird was still partially in the stone of the bailey and the defenders of Craig House still stood facing the possessed necromancer, who was now gathering purple lightnings around his hands in a manner similar to how Geoffrey called his own lightning, albeit more deliberately and elegantly.

Geoffrey. *Where is Geoffrey? And Bessariel? They were fighting zombies.*

However, the Dunstan-possessed necromancer seemed to be missing something. That something was important, somehow, and it nagged in memory at war with Zero's concern for his partners. *What's missing? The lines of thick purple energy that were feeding into the dual resurrectionists in one body aren't there anymore!* Zero realized with a start.

He pushed himself up to his feet, wobbling unsteadily, just as Geoffrey and Bessariel sprinted into the edge of sight.

"Oh, bother," said the dual necromancers, their voices in eerie chorus. To Zero, they commanded, "*You!* Deal with them!"

Zero had been subjected, however, on more than one occasion to the absolute will-crushing power of the Risen Tsar himself, and this time he wasn't caught by surprise by the possessed necromancer's attempt to subjugate him. Dunstan and his puppet necromancer were more powerful than any Zero had faced since escaping the Risen Tsar, but still only a fraction of that soul-controlling obscenity. Plus, he had the favour of the hawthorn and the rowan maidens and the blessed sun wheel of rowan twigs which he was just able to interpose between himself and the amplified power of the dual necromancers in one body. "Fuck you!" Zero growled. "And the resurrectionist you're riding in on! You're no Risen Tsar! I'm free of him and I'll be doubly-damned if I let some soul-riding leech of a bastard blood-magick-using resurrectionist order me around!" He took a step toward the possessed necromancer.

The necromancer's body jerked and almost lost control of the purple lightning it had been conjuring. "Call me a bastard, will you?!" snarled Dunstan's voice. "They can die, then! And you, necroknight, you'll pay for a *long* time. You and my father!"

The necromancer's purple lightning began to arch toward Zero's friends.

However, Zero was ready, already grabbing the necromancer's hands with his arcane seekers, just as he had grabbed small items and creatures many times before. Now he pulled desperately with every last bit of magick left to him, knowing he couldn't physically reach the dual necromancers in time. The lightnings slewed across the bailey, away from Bess and Geoff, barely missing the old Laird in his chains, but ending in a blinding ball of scintillating purple-black and oddly-golden light where the necroknight stood.

When Zero could see again, the afterimage of the sunwheel still lay over everything he saw. The rowan twigs were nothing now but ash across his fingers, but those fingers were still as intact as they had been before the lightnings struck him. The possessed necromancer was looking at him with something like fear in their eyes, while they used a semi-visible shield of sickly yellow energy, similar to the Laird's chains, to hold off Bessariel's attempts to savage them with her hooves and fangs.

Geoffrey seemed both scorched and stunned by the blast - while he remained on his feet, he wasn't moving except to blink and shake his head. But he was still standing and moving; Zero didn't think Geoff would have been had the necromancer's lightnings actually hit him.

Rowan and hawthorn petals drifted all around, joined by minuscule snowflakes as Zero drew what little warmth remained in the air to himself.

"Submit!" The possessed necromancer's eyes seemed to expand to fill all of Zero's vision. "You are *MINE!*"

The word thundered inside Zero's head, seeming to hang there in huge glowing letters. But the afterimage of the protective rowan sunwheel was still visible as well and Zero had years of suppressed memories and rage at being used as a killing puppet to draw on for strength to push Dunstan's demand aside.

"I don't talk to resurrectionists," Zero replied, his voice somewhat slurred and his tone disturbingly giddy.

He felt a curious floating detachment and a pressure as though he were drunk or had been drunk and was now on the edge of his worst hangover ever. "I don't belong to anyone except myself. And my horse. And she wants to eat you." Zero staggered across the few feet still separating him from the necromancer.

The necromancer could only try to angle the yellow shield, quickly learning he couldn't block both Bessariel and her partner coming at him from different directions.

"Go home, Dunstan. Go tell Ivan, I quit. I don't work for him any longer." Zero leaned in closer, his own arcane necromantic tendrils now starting to become visible and seeking contact with the living human on the other side of the annoying yellow shield. "I'm not going to work for you, either. Piss off!"

Bessariel squealed and struck at the necromancer again and the necromancer reflexively shifted the shield to block her.

The shield shifted just enough.

Zero was close enough for a wrap-around swing to put the blackthorn club into the side of the necromancer's stolen face, breaking bones and the connection between the possessing spirit of Dunstan and the unnamed lesser necromancer who was there in the flesh.

As soon as the terrible pressure in his head eased, Zero threw himself at the wounded necromancer. The blackthorn club connected again, Zero's attack driving the necromancer backward across frost-slicked ground.

"Never ever!" roared Zero and the blackthorn club swung up from ground level to snap the necromancer's head back and knock him from his feet.

"NEVER EVER AGAIN!"

Zero brought the club down on the necromancer several more times, until Bessariel and Geoffrey were suddenly beside him, steadying him before he threw himself on the still twitching body.

They herded him away from the possessed necromancer's body and the surviving defenders, over to the far edge of the crag's battlements.

And everything would have ended calmly then.

Would have, but for the geese which had escaped their confinement and been foraging among the stones with a supreme lack of concern for the battles around them.

One of the birds, almost as big as Zero was tall, came charging over - 'raaaah-onk!' - and bit Zero on the arm.

Both exhausted and exasperated necroknights and one seriously angry warmount turned on the offending goose and the rest of the flock.

The slaughter and the cloud of feathers were epic, worthy of a ballad.

***

"This is my demesne, child. And no unacknowledged bastard is going to come in here and take it," the laird said to the pummeled, smashed, and shredded remains of the necromancer, now lying in a stained drift of bloodied goose feathers. To everyone's relief, what was left of the body did not answer. Nor did Dunstan, from wherever he might have retreated to, choose to speak through the shattered body.

The old spectral warrior, still shaking off the remnants of the possessed necromancer's bindings, turned and started back toward his home. Passing the recovering necroknights, he jerked a thumb back at the bloody pile, "Burn that. Now!" He vanished again as he walked through the door of the Great House.

Zero looked at Geoffrey, who was blinking in surprise. "I think we'd better do what he said."

***

Morning came, as morning will while the world keeps turning. Zero was leaning back against Bessariel, as close to being asleep as was possible for a necroknight. The necromancer's pyre, built of the shattered defensive wall, had burnt down to embers. Separate pyres for the fallen defenders and for the horde of skeletons, zombies, and ghouls were still being prepared, but those jobs were being done by the humans who had been spared from the fighting.

Bennett was nearby, sharing a drink with Hrothgar, Geoffrey, and Bridget.

"So, does that mean the old laird is actually a banshee?" Bennett was asking.

"In the Scottish Highlands," said Hrothgar in reply, "you can't tell the difference between ancestral ghosts and elves."

Bridget added, "That's because some of our ancestral ghosts *are* elves."

Zero snorted and even Geoffrey couldn't hide a grin. "Truth," he said. "Though the old Laird Craig seems human enough."

***

Later, as Zero was lingering on the ramparts, the spectral laird appeared beside him and said, "Have that sorry excuse for a priest come up here and say a mass for our souls. But not until after they've dug my mortal remains out of the rubble, mind you. And have him say one for anyone else they might find in there as well.

Though no one else stayed to keep the guard with me, it's the proper thing to do. Anglicans can still say Mass, can't they?"

"I've no idea," said Zero. "I gave sacrifice to Cian and Lugh and honor to the rest of the Tuatha when I was still breathing. But I don't think the Scottish Kirk is Anglican. They'll certainly have rites for the dead, though."

"Well, find out then, you heathen. Or I just might decide to haunt you for the rest of your days."

Zero hid a smile and touched his hat brim in salute.

10: CLEANING THE CEMETERY

"Don't you two have anything better to do than sit around decomposing?"

Zerollen diGriz tilted his head back and eyed the Caliburn knight who'd spoken. The small necroknight had been watching his black mare Bessariel cropping the greening spring grass beside the older warmount Broken Sky. Both warmounts were grazing among what was now Invercraig's horse herd, formerly belonging to the outlaw company who had tried to take over the village.

"We're doing something useful," he explained. "We're keeping an eye on the stock in case of reivers."

He shifted higher on the lichen-decorated stone he'd been lounging against. "We're out of the way. We're not scare-ing" - he drew out the word as though it were two separate ones with more than a hint of sarcasm - "anyone. What do you think we *should* be doing, Bennett?"

The Caliburn knight ran a hand through their curly copper-brown hair, but chose not to rise to Zero's baiting, understanding why their friend was being more irritable and contrary than usual. "Dand Woodward would like to have words with you."

"Regarding what? Those damned geese, again? And who might Dand Woodward be, to be bothering us about that?"

"He'd be the local vicar of the Scottish Kirk. But it isn't about the geese, Zero. Not directly, at least."

"What are we being accused of now?" asked Zerollen's squire, Geoffrey Hartsbane, from the other side of the boulder.

Zero sighed and sat up. "I'll go find out, Geoff." Turning to Bennett, he asked, "They don't like to be called priests, do they?"

"No," said Bennett. "Though you could call him Father Woodward if you want to be polite."

Zero quirked the remains of a battered eyebrow at Bennet. "Why would I possibly want to do that?" He picked up his wide-brimmed hat decked with hawthorn bloom and rowan - an odd mixture made moreso by the fact the rowan was also blooming quite before its season - and plopped it onto his head, hiding his expression from the standing knight.

Geoffrey snorted and chuckled rustily from the grass on the other side of the stone.

Bennett frowned at both of the necroknights. "Might save you from getting an unnecessary blast of God's Grace."

"Who's to say it would be unnecessary?" muttered Geoffrey. "Want me to come along?"

"Stay. After the show we put on with the resurrectionist and the great goose slaughter, I think we're better off only giving them one of us at a time. And I'm less intimidating than you."

"More fools, they, if they actually think that about you," said Geoffrey.

***

"Goodwife MacLaine came to me yesterday," Father Dand Woodward explained, "about her daughter

Chritiana being out with the remnants of their goose flock -"

"I knew those geese were involved in this, somehow," Zero said aloud.

"Shush!" said Bennett.

The vicar exchanged glances with the Caliburn knight and continued as though the interruption hadn't occurred. " – and seeing will o' wisps flitting about the old battlefield cemetery. I'd like your help to investigate and re-consecrate the ground."

"It *is* something in need of doing," Zero admitted reluctantly. He had been planning a visit to the cemetery in the dale, but the incident with the geese after the battle for Craig House had almost pushed it out of his mind. Nor were his plans for the ancient boneyard something he'd really wanted to have the young cleric involved in, but Zero knew he certainly didn't have the ability to purify a cemetery in a way the locals would find acceptable. "Not waiting until we're finding ourselves up to our hips in skeletons again is probably a good idea as well. What do you want done?"

"Keeping the skeletons we might find there from eating me while I do the purification rituals comes first to my mind," Father Woodward dryly.

"T'ha!" Zero snorted a laugh. "I think we might be useful in that case."

Sobering, he added, "But we'll make sure you have a good mount who isn't wind-broken before we set out. And if I tell you to run, you run."

"Which would work up to the point where I'm actually doing the ceremony," the vicar agreed. "Once I'm started though, you'll need to keep things from attacking me."

"Then we'll need to plan on scouting the area well before you start. Best we plan for several days out there, even if we only need it for the weather."

"Do you think you'd be able to secure any more rowan?" Father Woodward ask, gesturing toward the blooms on Zero's hat.

"Not blooming," Zero said shortly, leaning back from the man. He broke the uncomfortable pause by adding, "But if you've got rowan growing in the churchyard or your cemetery, you might tell the trees what you need it for and see if they drop any twigs or branches. If you don't have rowan there, possibly someone in the village has some growing."

"Speak with the trees?" The young vicar looked more puzzled than doubtful to Zero's eyes.

"Tell them what you're planning on doing and if they agree, you'll likely find it. Or not. It's like praying, sometimes it works, sometimes it doesn't. Or not immediately.

***

"See? You can speak nicely with the clergy when you choose to," said Bennett.

"Its usually not worth the effort," Zero replied. "But that one has promise, if he can avoid having some old fool accuse him of witchcraft or dealing with one of their devils for talking to me."

"You wouldn't have any one in mind for doing that, wouldn't you?" Bennett pressed him.

Zero tilted his head to look at the Caliburn knight. "Oh, at least one," he admitted. "Possibly more."

"You're hardly an optimist, Zero."

He nodded. "I've been around long enough to know humans will be offered two possibilities and will choose the worst of the two more often than not. Elves do it as well, if they don't stop and think about it. And sometimes you don't have time and just have to do something."

Doing something on Zero's part involved buying salt and jugs for water and several small swatches of netting to wrap the jugs in to keep them from clinking together. Bennett had brought his monthly pay from Thornhill and a letter from the garrison commander authorizing his time on detached duty 'for rest and recovery as needed'; that there'd been another letter — authorizing Bennett to pay for his pyre and elven graces said if his body could be recovered — wasn't spoken of between them. He picked up a bottle of ink, parchment as Invercraig's shops had no paper in stock, and new quills. Bennett bought some parchment as well, for their and Hrothgar's reports.

"When are you heading back to Thornhill?" Zero asked as they left the shop.

"That depends on whether we can flag down a courier or one of us has to take them north." Bennett ran a hand through their curls. "We'll be writing our reports and requisitions tonight, then probably tossing a coin to see who takes them. I've put the flag up on the inn's sign and one down at the stable today in case a rider comes through. We're more than due for one and it would be a pleasure to send things out rather than making that ride again so soon."

"We'll be having people coming in from the nearby towns to see if the place is still standing quick enough." Zero glanced at the bundle of goods. "I need to send Sir Tercel and Warmaster Icewraith notes about Geoffrey and what I plan on doing about that resurrectionist. I'm of two minds about taking Geoff with me on this trip with Father Woodward," he admitted as they walked toward the inn. "He'd be a help in a fight, but if we run into Dunstan again . . ."

"You'd rather not risk him?" Bennett asked, knowingly.

"You know me too well, Bennett," Zero replied darkly. "Dunstan almost broke me during the battle and he wasn't there with access to all of his abilities."

"And you were exhausted from fighting all night," Bennett pointed out. "Dunstan might not even be a problem any longer, after what you and Laird Craig did to him and his host body."

"I'm not sure I'd bet on that," Zero paused outside the door to the inn. "If you don't have a body or a pile of dust –"

"- they could be halfway to Port Royal by now," Bennett finished. "I know. Will we see the two of you here tonight?"

"We might drop in, but more likely we'll be up at the Great House preparing for the ride out to the old battlefield. Would you please make sure we'll have good horses for Woodward and Geoff? That bay mare tolerates him well, but if you can find another? I'd rather not keep using the same horses after what happened with Lazy Lob."

"I can do that," Bennett said. "Until later, then, old friend."

"Until later," Zero nodded and turned toward Craig House. A spring burbled up in the lowest level of the House, filling a well before the excess was channeled out to the bailey and from there ran out a culvert in the remains of the wall to drain down into the dale below. The well itself would provide the pure water he wanted for any ceremonies he might need to do himself or hand off to Dand Woodward for the young priest to bless – *Priest? No, this one's a vicar, which is another flavor of priest*, Zero reminded himself. There were enough blackthorn sloe in the dale to ensure he could glean some of their fallen twigs for the sort of incense he might use.

Geoffrey found him later at the far end of the great hall, seated at a decorative table he'd weaseled out of the smaller room beyond.

Zero had laid aside his hat and leaned over the tiny table, scratching away at a sheet of parchment with a goose-quill pen in the elven style of bottom right to upper left script, muttering to himself about verb endings in Latin and occasionally breaking into snatches of song. He'd pulled a chair out of the other room as well, and perched on it, one foot swinging restlessly as he wrote.

The tall necroknight paused by the fireplace, stuck by how much like a youth at his studies his partner looked in the moment.

Then Zero glanced up, the arcane blue of his eyes gleaming in the shadows. "Ah, you've found me," he said, setting his pen aside and sliding down off the chair to greet his companion. "Ready to go on an adventure? Or would you rather stay here to flirt with Bridget Greneglais?"

"Eh!" said Geoff in surprise. "No! Stop that, Zero! That's just not right."

"Sorry, Geoff," Zero told him. "I have not manners at times."

"Only at times?" Geoff smirked. "What's this adventure? I see you seem to have escaped talking with the vicar without losing any more pieces of yourself."

Zero's expression changed and he reached up suddenly and tapped the sides of his head. "Ears are still here," he sighed in relief, startling Geoffrey further.

"Why wouldn't they be?"

"Never mind. Uw'zekal sewed them back on for me." Zero shuddered and seemed to refocus on his partner. "Have I ever mentioned how much I hate doing paperwork?"

"Not until now. What is all this?"

"Reports to the Caliburn Knights and the Knights of the Red Horse, letting everyone know I'm still walking around and what I'll be working on over the next few months. And letting them know about you. That should raise a few eyebrows. And a few hackles."

"I take it they won't be happy about me?"

"They'll get over it." Zero picked up one of the pages, holding it to the light. Satisfied with whatever he saw, he rolled the parchment tightly and tucked it under an arm, while he pulled out sealing wax and twine to finish closing the roll. "After all, Sir Davidson didn't forbid me from using my full powers. Nor did Her Majesty. Or Warmaster Icewraith."

"Seriously?" Geoffrey looked abashed. "You move in some elevated circles, Sir Zerollen."

"No! Don't you dare call me that, not in that way, Geoff!" Zero dropped the scroll and rushed over to the other necroknight. "I'm just Zero. Just a hell-raiser from the Debatable Lands, Geoffrey. Not some lord putting on airs along with his hose and lace. Circumstances threw me in with the nobles, yes, but it doesn't make me one of them."

"Are you reading my mind?" Geoff asked a trifle shakily.

"No," Zero told him. "But I've been where you are now, when I came back to myself and felt unworthy to even exist. Remember when you asked me if this was a second chance? Maybe it is. An extraordinary chance and it puts us in some extraordinary positions, in contact with some of the other uncommon personages of the world. We're Knights, Geoff. It isn't just a mockery of the title. We're Free Undead and we stand against not only those who would control us, but against everything undead are created to be. We are worthy to hold our heads high before nobles or royals because we have free will and the right to choose our path in this world, just as the living do. Never forget that!"

He tapped Geoffrey on the chest. "I named you as a knight and when we finally get to Thornhill or another stronghold of our order, you'll be formally knighted. Never forget, though," he tapped Geoff on the chest again. "It's what's in here and here," he touched his own head, since Geoff's was out of easy reach, "which makes us knights. The ceremony only confirms it."

The taller knight let out a sigh of relief. "I really wasn't sure, even though the Caliburns seemed comfortable with you calling me Sir Geoffrey." He shook his head, "It still feels odd to consider myself a knight."

Zerollen chuckled. "One of the other names for our Order is the Knights Irregular, though the Hapsburgers are more inclined to use that term, when they don't use something more descriptive, but less appealing.

"We have members riding under the Empire's banner?"

"Oh, yes. Ivan wasn't particular about who he conscripted into his army. Some of our brothers and sisters in death are in service in the Hapsburg Empire. Remember me mentioning other necroknights could be a danger to you? If you meet them on the battlefield, those who returned to their homelands in the Empire almost certainly will be. But let me get these ready to send, since it sounds like Bennett or Hrothgar will be taking them north unless we had a courier come through today."

***

Much to their surprise, there was a courier at the Salmon, bringing the townsfolk up to date on the latest news from the south and getting the news of the attack on Invercraig as well. Hrothgar had been near the door. Zero managed to catch his eye and pass off the reports without having to go inside the crowded public house.

"We'll be up to Craig House in the morning to brief you on any news of interest from the south. So far, it does sound like there has been an outbreak of measles in all the towns north of Invar Nis," the Danish knight told him. "I think there might be more to the tale the courier is spinning, but there are too many here to speak freely. We will question him later, when the crowd is gone."

Hrothgar scratched at something in his mustache, then added, "Bennett has mounts for the Vicar Woodward and Sir Geoffrey. She said to tell you she couldn't get a replacement for the bay mare."

"Fuck!" said Zero loudly.

"What's wrong?" Geoff asked from behind him.

Several other people were glancing their way, attracted by Zero's outburst. "See you in the morning, Hrothgar," the small necroknight said hastily and pulled the pub door shut again before starting blindly back the road.

"Zero?" Geoff hurried after his companion, who was already striding back toward Craig House.

Zero growled warningly in reply, then shook himself. "I was hoping we could find you another horse, if you're coming with us tomorrow," he explained, still walking fast for the outskirts of Invercraig.

"Why wouldn't I? And why do I need to change horses? I like the bay."

"She's a good horse," said Zero. "I don't want her to end up wheezing and wind-broke like Lazy Lob."

"What? You've lost me, what are you talking about?"

"Lob broke down on me during the run from the ghoul pack. I'd rather not damage another horse by keeping her around us on a regular basis."

"Wait," Geoff stopped just outside the village wall. "You think we made that horse you've been riding sick? Zero, he was wind broke when Dyer's horse buyer picked him up for the company back in Invar Nis. That horse dealer pulled one over on us with your chestnut. The rest of the horses we got for remounts weren't bad, so we didn't go back and take our money out of the seller's hide when we found out he couldn't do more than a slow trot for any length of time."

Now it was Zero's turn to be surprised. "You're sure?"

"Yes, I'm sure. Despite what some of the villagers might think and apparently, what you think as well, you don't go around with a cloud of sickness hanging over you. If either of us seems likely to be spreading disease, it would be me, Zerollen. And I don't see myself doing that, except when we were fighting the skeletons and you did whatever you did and released all my powers."

Geoff started walking again, "You're going to have to explain why I don't call ice out of nowhere like you do, but even before the fight, I was seeing things, like the actual cloud around Agnes and Mary-wee when they were so sick." A strand of his long, pale hair blew across his eyes and he brushed it back over his shoulder. "Then I … I pulled for ice like I'd seen? Felt? Felt you do, but instead I got those midges which rotted the ghouls' weapons and the skeletons' bones. What the hell was that, Zero?"

Zero turned their path down to the beach from the coastal road. Looking out at the waves lapping silver-edged lace along the sand, he explained, "You have power over sicknesses and decay, Geoff. Either from how you died or passed on by whoever tainted you originally. Its part of you the way the ice is part of me now."

Geoff turned his face up to the stars. "Well, then, it's all new to me, but I'm sure you can trust me on this, Zero. You didn't do anything to Lazy Lob, except make him work harder for you than he'd had to up until that point."

"Thank you, Geoff."

The two necroknights continued watching the water until the rising wind and wind-lifted sand made standing there more uncomfortable than they were willing to tolerate. They climbed the switchback road up to Craig House and checked on the children before beginning to pack for their morning trip. Now that one of the necromancers was dead for certain and the others seemed dead or driven off, Aggie and Mary-wee and several others who had been very sick seemed to be responding to Bridget's medicines and were already noticeably recovering.

***

After wishing Hector and Broken Sky luck in watching over Hector's sisters, they set out for the old battleground and the cemetery near it. Dand Woodward joined the pair of necroknights at the bottom of the switchback up to Craig House. He rode a dark bay gelding who seemed happy to tag along with the two mares, even if one of them was a warmount. The gelding was less pleased to be in the company of the necroknights, snorting and sidling away whenever he caught their scent. Since the vicar Father Woodward handled the nervous horse well enough, Zero decided not to comment on the matter and enjoy as much of the ride as he could.

The group took the lane past the Mackintoshes' large holding. Some of the family were already back at the farm, doing repairs and otherwise going about the work necessary before the spring planting could start, though most were still encamped at Craig House until the dale was declared clear of roaming undead.

Old Maeve MacLaine's brother-in-law Tam and his wife were back at their cottage with their sheep. Maeve, and Maeve's daughter Chrita, and her granddaughter Chritiana the goosegirl had returned to their own small holding as well. They stopped there for a late morning break and Zero surprised the women by giving them what remained of his stipend. They would have turned down the money, until Zero pointed out, "We ate your geese, goodwives, even if never they saw the table. It is only right I pay you for them." He had a little coin still set aside for the MacKintosh goose boy as well, when he had time to seek the lad out.

Beyond the MacLaines' the lane turned into a path through their small fields, then to a trace easily mistaken for a game trail, but for the recent passage of the ghouls and skeletons the necromancer had summoned. The undead had churned up the ground enough to have made a muddy mess of the trace itself. The zombie trail had veered off into the pasture land closer to the crag where Craig House perched rather than the undead having taken the more direct lane beyond the MacLaines' farm on their way to the coast. "That seems odd," Geoff said.

Father Woodward agreed.

"We'll see what might be along there on our way back," Zero said. "Let's see if there's anything we still need to worry about out here first, since we've already come this far." But before he led them further toward the cemetery, he urged Bessariel along the side trail until he felt he was far enough away from the young vicar and his skittish horse to send seekers probing the disturbed ground. He found only the faintest traces of unnatural passage out to the limit of his scanning, nothing sunlight and rain wouldn't clear within a few more days' time.

Well off the sides of the undead's path, the bright tips of elder and the first suggestion of the fiddleheads of bracken poked out of the undamaged soil and a tinge of green through the petals of the blackthorns hinted the leaves were thinking of budding. The land would soon recover, unlike some of the places he had seen where the Risen had poisoned the countryside with their passage.

Returning from his scouting, Zero rejoined Geoff and the vicar. Not much later, the three came at last to the farthest part of the dale the necroknights had previously explored.

The cemetery walls still stood in the distance, surrounded by the copse of ancient yew and hawthorn, though no host of undead stood among the remaining grave markers as they had on the necroknights' original visit. The thorn trees here were only beginning to blossom, but their distinctive smell was stronger, as though held in by the larger trees. A faint underlying scent of turned earth was on the air as well, but it was nothing like the smell which had greeted the pair of knights the first time they had been here.

Father Woodward's gelding didn't seem particularly concerned by the smells and a day of being in relatively close contact with the necroknights had relieved much of his earlier skittishness. The vicar rode up to join Zero and Geoff when nothing untoward appeared out of the cemetery or surrounding trees.

"Stay here," Zero told him. "Geoff, you take the right side, we'll circle around to see if there's anything on the other side of the walls."

Bessariel chose a path outside the thin hedge of blackthorn and yew, occasionally dropping her head down to sniff the ground while Zero watched for movement from both within and without the cemetery wall. Nothing other than small birds and wood mice seemed active in the tall weeds beyond the mown area which extended perhaps half a bow shot around the walls.

"Anything?" Zero asked Geoffrey when they met on the far side of cemetery.

"Nothing so far," said Geoff. He looked across the graveyard and added, "It's actually clearer here than back in Invercraig."

"Probably a good sign." Zero leaned back and stretched. "Nothing out here for sickness to be clinging to, unlike somewhere with living people. Though I'm rather surprised one of the resurrectionists didn't blight something. They're a spiteful lot."

"Other than having us show up, maybe nothing here annoyed them."

"I wish we didn't have to be talking like there was more than one of those bastards unaccounted for. See you around the other side."

Geoff nodded and clicked to his bay mare. Bessariel stood still a moment longer, staring into the forest beyond the old field.

"What?" Zero asked her.

The black warmount shook her head and reached back to nibble fondly at Zero's boot before starting off around the walls again.

A trail led toward the forest, not far beyond where they had stopped in their circling. Zero turned Bess down the path for a few strides and sent forth his probes as he had at the undead's trail earlier in the day. This time he found no traces of undead, though there was an odd arcane flicker among the winter-browned grasses, as though something of power had moved through them.

The riders regrouped back with Father Woodward.

"Anything?" the vicar asked. "Nothing seems to be happening here."

"I didn't see or sense anything," Geoffrey told him.

Bessariel bowed, letting her rider dismount more easily, then rose and gave herself a good shake. "I know, lovely one," Zero told her, unstrapping his supplies from behind her saddle.

Setting the supplies aside, he turned to the task of unbuckling Bess's saddle and removing it, then slipping her bitless bridle off. Looking up at his still-mounted companions, Zero added, "There's something odd about the path into the forest, but nothing within the last couple of days. Anything of the arcane which was done here is either within the graveyard or mostly dissipated. Let's make camp and something hot to drink, then we can start exploring inside."

Bess wandered out into the unmown field, sniffing around rather like a large dog until she found a place she favored to lie down and roll in. The other two riders seemed to take their cue it was safe to dismount from Bessariel's behavior and got off their horses as well.

Zero continued as he pulled a frost-raised stone loose and set it in place to start building a fire ring, "I didn't see anything to suggest the resurrectionists had any luck raising the dead outside the cemetery."

"Why do you think that is?" Father Woodward asked, removing his own supplies and saddle from his gelding. "I'd heard there was a battle fought out here long ago. Might there not have been enough left to raise?"

"Can't say for certain," Zero called from where he was building the spot for a cookfire. "But I'd guess the dead were gathered in piles in the area the cemetery covers now. Clearly, this was long before we all began burning our dead. I've a suspicion the stones used for the cairns over the dead were what were taken to make the walls we see now."

"That doesn't sound like it was the wisest of ideas to me," said Geoffrey, pulling rope for a stakeout line for the horses from his saddlebags.

"It probably wasn't," said Father Woodward. "It likely would have been better to leave the cairns undisturbed and bring in stones from elsewhere in the fields."

"Unfortunately, not everyone has that much wisdom, especially when faced with the amount of work constructing those walls likely took." Having said that, Zero returned to prepping the area and the kettle, while Geoffrey and Father Woodward finished swapping their horses' bridles for halters and tied the more likely to stray beasts to their grazing lines.

The small necroknight, finally satisfied he'd cleared enough space to avoid starting a grass fire, pulled one of the cutdown squares of peat he carried in place of dried rations out of his saddlebags, dug his flint and steel from another part of the bags, and coaxed a fire into starting.

Geoffrey had foraged out into the heavier brush and came back with an armful of wood to add to their supply. "Pity we can't glean anything from under the yews, but that's likely all poisonous."

"I'm surprised to see the hawthorn growing among the yews. Usually nothing grows under the shadow of yew," agreed Father Woodward.

"Look how they're planted," Zero gestured with his mug toward the trees. The thorns are just out of the yews' rainshadow when you look down to where their roots likely grow in the earth. Someone had thought about how they'd grow over the years and planted them with care. There's nothing random about how the bigger ones were placed."

"You think they were placed there for protection?"

"Almost certainly," Zero agreed. "The question is, to keep things out? Or to keep things in?"

"Perhaps both?" Geoff suggested.

"Possibly."

"We'll likely know soon enough," said Zero, reaching over to take the kettle off the fire and pour all of them hot drinks.

After the necroknights were warmer and Father Woodward had a bit of cheese and bread in addition to his tea, they banked their fire, gathered what equipment they might immediately need, and approached the walled cemetery. The walls were broken in only one place and this by a stile wide enough a coffin could be carried up the steep steps and down into the yard itself.

From the top of the stile, they could easily see where the earth had been turned over in wide swaths, almost as if someone had taken a plow to the ground. Slabs of stone had been roughly pushed aside, uprooted, or knocked sideways and what plants had grown within the walls were trampled into the mud. Most seemed to be dying.

Most, but not all. Near one corner - Zero thought it might be the one closest to where the old military road ran - was a small bushy yew and under it, an even smaller boxy stack of stone where moss and lichen still grew undisturbed. He threw out his arms to block Geoff and Father Woodward from going further.

"Wait!" he warned. He took only enough steps forward to protect the living human from his seekers as he probed the graveyard. Even before sending them out, he could feel there was something within the walls watching them.

The taint of the undead lingered in the furrows and on the broken, displaced stones, but only in the shades of purple Zero was familiar with from power similar to his own. Thankfully, there seemed to be no spots of red or sickly yellow-green to show where the land was desecrated or poisoned.

As he probed toward the undamaged corner, he suddenly encountered a barrier which flashed brilliant blue, mixed with the true golden light of pure spirit. With a yelp of surprise and pain, he dropped his probes, throwing up an arcane shield over himself and his companions reflexively. Across the desecrated graveyard, a huge wolfish dog, easily as big as a calf, and with eyes as arcanely blue as a necroknight's, stepped out of nowhere much as Bessariel did when leaving the Hidden Ways, and raced toward them, barking fiercely.

Behind the dog came a woman yelling in a mixture of Gàidhlig and Pictish Zero could barely understand.

"Don't attack them!" he managed to warn his companions before either of them did more than begin defensive actions.

Unlike his first meeting with Bannock, the huge black dog didn't try to bite him, but it kept up a ferocious baying until Bessariel appeared at the top of the steps and screamed a warmount's warning back at the beast. The woman had caught up to the dog by then and both parties stared at each other across the open space remaining between them.

Without the dog bellowing, it was easier to hear the woman, but still difficult for Zero to understand her.

"What's she saying?" asked Father Woodward.

"It seems to be variations on get out and stay out, with curses thrown in," Zero told him. "But she's speaking a variant dialect I've not heard before. She could just as easily be inviting us to dinner, but I strongly doubt that's what she's saying."

"Can you tell her why we're here?"

"I can try." He looked back at the woman and added, over his shoulder, "Geoff, you and Dand should back up at least to the riser just on the other side of the top of the stairs. I think she's faire chlaidh - keeping the watch, that is. And she's strong on her own ground, likely far stronger than I am. And she has a grim with her. Get yourselves on the other side of the threshold. You too, Bess."

The warmount snorted a laugh and came further down the stairs, leaving Geoff and Father Woodward scant room to make their retreat. She loomed protectively over Zero, upper lip drawn back to show her fangs.

"Thank the Almighty, she's not as wide as the other one," exclaimed the vicar as he scrambled over the crest of the stairs, presumably in reference to Broken Sky.

"Eak shee!" said the guardian woman. The huge dog growled, but sat down.

"Warmount," corrected Zero. "Can you understand me?"

It took some swapping between languages, but eventually they ended up speaking more elven than anything else. The woman, as Zero had suspected, was the last to have been buried in the graveyard and was bound to linger until another was buried there and could take up the watch. The grim — the black dog — had been there even longer, bound since the building of the wall around the burial area to protect the place and any spirits which had lingered. They had fought the necromancer, fought, and been driven back to their own small part of the cemetery. The rest of the cemetery had been emptied, except for a few other spirits who remained who had been powerful enough *and* bound strongly enough to their graves to resist the necromancers.

There had been three of those dark twisted mages according to the woman, one a ghoul, one who sounded from her description to be the possessed necromancer who Zero had destroyed at Craig House. The third and most powerful was likely Dunstan, though the woman had never seen more of him than a cloaked figure riding something which might have been a horse once upon a time. As best the woman could tell, he had left with the ghoul necromancer sometime before Zero and Geoffrey had first approached the cemetery, by perhaps as much as a day or more.

She wanted to know why Zero and the others had come, but was less pleased with what Father Woodward intended to do. By then, it was late enough in the day the few other remaining spirits were beginning to manifest and each of them also had opinions on whether they wanted their burial places consecrated to the deity the vicar served.

They were also somewhere between being fascinated and horrified by Zero and his 'condition,' as one of them put it.

Eventually, Bessariel lowered her head and bunted him with her nose. "What?" Zero asked.

She huffed warm breath over him and he realized just how cold he'd been getting, sitting there and talking with the dead.

"I have to go hunt," he told them. "Or I won't be safe for the living to be around."

"You'll come back?"

"You won't leave us to that priest, will you?"

It took a bit to calm the spirits, but he was eventually able to get away. Geoffrey had his mug full of hot, salted water ready for him at the bottom of the stile. But even his squire backed away from the cold which seemed to center around Zero.

"I have to go hunt," he warned Geoff. "Try to keep Father Woodward from doing anything to the graves until I get back."

"I'll do what I can, Zero. Are you going to be alright?"

"I need to find a stag or something similar. I'll be back once I've found something to eat. You should hunt too. We're going to need our strength for what comes next."

***

What came next was talking Dand Woodward into only consecrating part of the cemetery.

Zero had come back to camp in the middle of the night with a red deer doe slung over Bessariel's back and a haunted expression he didn't explain to Geoffrey.

The young vicar had been up late into the night as well, praying for guidance after having watched and listened to Zero talking with the ghosts in the graveyard. He was still deeply asleep when Geoffrey started heating water as dawn began filtering through the clouds.

Zero joined Geoff for a mug of water by the fire after he'd shifted the horses' picket line to allow them more grazing. Bess, her muzzle still stained from the hunt, followed him and lay down near the fire, providing her rider with a warm backrest and wind-block while Geoffrey filled Zero in on what had happened and not happened at the camp before he'd gotten back. Then Zero had a short language lesson with his squire before Father Woodward woke up to the smell of venison drying on a makeshift rack near the fire.

The argument over how the consecration would be done began almost immediately and dragged on for over an hour before Zero's patience finally wore thin. "For the last time, no! There are beings there who have been there since before your religion existed. You will not force them out or do something to make their existence there painful. Being bound is bad enough –"

"Would it not be better for them to be freed? I had understood you necroknights prize free will above everything else."

"You are missing the point," Zero said, standing up. "None of them asked to be sent on, not even the woman standing watch. They want to stay or think they deserve to stay. Any who didn't and were strong enough to defy the resurrectionists are already gone. If you really want to debate their self-chosen penance with them, you are quite welcome to walk in there this evening and discuss it with them. If you can. I will *not* be translating."

Zero glared down at the still seated vicar. "The Old Church," he said, referring to the Roman Catholics, "had places in its cemeteries for the unbaptized, the suicides, and the excommunicated. Don't try telling me yours does not."

"Those aren't usually allowed within the walls on holy ground," Father Woodward said stiffly.

"Walls and holy ground is it? Which you create by consecrating the ground. We can make allowances for that, then." Zero turned and dodged around Bessariel, heading for the cemetery. "Come on, Geoff. I'm going to need your help with this!"

"What are you planning on doing?"

"You want walls, vicar? We're going to make you walls!"

Father Woodward got an object lesson in just how strong necroknights were, as Zero and Geoffrey shifted stone slabs and broken tombstones most of the morning, creating what was more a fence than a wall between the areas where early Christians had been laid to rest next to older burials. Damaged graves still inhabited were restored to the limit of the knights' skill, with the vicar coming to help with more recently created resting places. They heard the black dog panting and padding about, but it didn't manifest enough to be seen and none of the other inhabitants made immediate objections.

They spent a good hour building the gateway between the two sections, then broke for lunch for the vicar and for the last of the energy the two necroknights could draw from the doe's carcass and mugs of hot salted water.

Geoffrey led them to a spring he'd found at the farthest edge of the old field and all of them washed in the chill water.

Father Woodward changed clothing. When they returned to camp, he'd asked, "If there are no further objections?" Hearing none, he put on the more formal vestments of his office, spoke a blessing over the items he required and set out to finally re-consecrate the part of the cemetery set aside for the dead of similar beliefs to his own.

Geoffrey, who was or at least had been, of a Christian faith himself, stayed closer to Dand Woodward, to protect him from any last minute objections from anyone or anything inside or out of the graveyard. Meanwhile, Zero, mounted on Bessariel, kept watch over the area from the relative high ground of the stile over the wall. The ceremony was elegant and came off without interruption.

Zero and Bessariel felt the threshold form around that section of the cemetery as a gentle pressure pushing them back and to the side. The black warmount shuffled sideways a step on top of the stile, but otherwise refused to be forced from the entrance. They waited until Father Woodward and Geoffrey had climbed the wide stile and left the cemetery before the mare pivoted and brought her rider safely down.

"Keep the vicar safe," Zero told his squire before leaving to start his part of the reconsecration of the graveyard.

Bessariel cantered around to the northernmost point of the walls, where Zero unloaded the sea salt and spring water he'd brought with him onto the wall, before swinging off Bess's back onto the wall himself. He heard the Grim grumbling to itself and felt the attention of the spirits who had chosen to remain.

"I'd never be accused of being a priest," he said aloud as he prepared for the working. "Or a mage. But I was and am a soldier and I've taken part in pyres and burials entirely more times than I care to think on. I'll try to remember the patterns and give what protection and honor to you and your resting place as I can."

He lit a candle, whispered a prayer to those he personally followed, drew his sword, and sketched a symbol of the Powers of the North as much in his mind's eye as in the air. Holding his blade crossbody to give his arm extra support, he turned carefully atop the wall and began walking deosil – sunward. When he came to where the other half of the graveyard began, where he could feel, if not see, the protection already there, he jumped down with surprising grace, turning to pace along the line of the fence he and Geoffrey had created. When he reached what felt like the eastern midpoint through the link he shared with Bessariel, he stopped and lit another candle, drew another shape on the air and in his mind with his blade, and continued thusly until he reached the stile and was able to gain the top of the original walls again.

He repeated the circles twice more, once sprinkling the sea salt, and once with the spring water, singing the greetings to the Powers at each cardinal point with more certainty each time, singing in a stronger, deeper voice than would be expected from someone of his stature. Returning to his northern starting point, he called out, “Let nothing of evil or malicious intent disturb this holy circle!”

Faintly, from the corner of his eye, he saw a golden line wink into being and the suggestion of a symbol shimmer in the colors of the North. Before he could turn his head to see if the line continued or other symbols became visible, there was an audible note and as he turned, for a moment he saw golden light radiating skyward from the entire wall. It rose up as well from those graves he knew had still been occupied and he heard a sound like the whistling passing of some great flock of geese or swans overhead.

Then the light was gone, but the Grim stood with its forefeet on the wall beside him, eyes gleaming the rich green of growing things. It licked his hand and then vanished again into the growing evening shadows.

“Go now to Your Own Places,” Zero whispered to the watching Powers he had summoned in his mother’s language, “and let there be no ill will between me and Thee.”

His fingers burned as though he'd thrust them into flame and the tip of his sword still shimmered with the faintest trace of gold.

Abruptly, it was more than he could deal with and he sank down beside the still-burning candle, sobbing for the beauty of what he had seen and heard.

Sobbing, also, for once again being left behind.

Then Bessariel and Geoffrey reached him, the tall necroknight vaulting up onto the wall beside Zero and hugging him fiercely, his warmount leaning her dark head against him. They stayed that way until the skies cleared and moonlight shone down on the purified graveyard, letting them find their way back around to the comfort of the camp fire and fresh hares Father Woodward had collected from snares Geoffrey had set the previous night.

***

In the morning, they washed and ate their varied breakfasts, collected the last of their items, took down the snares, and began the ride back to Invercraig. Though they took the undead's path along the edge of the mountain until it joined at the Narrows with the sea, they found nothing to fully explain why the skeletons and ghouls had bypassed most of the dale's farms.

"All I can imagine," suggested Father Woodward, "is the necromancer knew there was an escape tunnel, but didn't know exactly where it was."

"Good for all of us," said Zero, coming back from checking where the undead had veered all the way to the steep hillside and appeared to have dug about for some uncertain amount of time. Zero had found nothing and no indication anything had either been taken or left behind. Though it would have been hard to tell if anything had been taken, unless it had been an item of enough taint or arcane energy for him to detect.

The dale seemed greener than when they had ridden out, the grass flush with new sprouts and the bushes and trees when seen at a distance seeming surrounded by a green mist.

The sun was out by the time they reached the switchback up to Craig House. The necroknights parted from the young vicar at the great house's stable. Once they'd freed the horses and Bessariel from their tack, they left their gear at the stable and herded the two mortal horses back down the road to where the town's now sizable herd grazed in the open fields near the MacKintosh steading.

There was a steep and very fresh path which might have been created by those ghouls which had broken the necromancer's control and fled the battle for Craig House leading down from the great house road. Even the desire to check in on their orphans was muted by the opportunity to simply be still, be warm, and not have another emergency immediately demanding their attention. It was too good a moment to let pass.

Zero and Geoffrey found a sunlit boulder near the path and stretched out there, enjoying the momentary quiet and escape from having living humans constantly around them. Bessariel went to graze with the horses and exchange whatever gossip warmounts shared with each other with Broken Sky, who was keeping the herd from scattering too far out into the dale.

11: FAMILY MATTERS

Some indeterminate time later, a familiar voice broke in on their reverie, "Oh, thank Saints George and Aindreas! There you are!"

Zero started up, scanning the immediate area and the fields for threats, one hand on his sword, the other on the blackthorn club he carried instead of a mace. "What? What's gone wrong now?"

"What do we have to do now, Bennett?" Geoffrey asked, sounding less alarmed, but equally annoyed.

"Prepare to defend your charges from that Deacon Fraiser and several others who seem to want the MacLeans' farm. They're having a meeting about the children's future right now."

"They're *what*?" Zero rolled over and started getting up. Beside him, his accidental squire sat up and rolled to his feet as well. Both necroknights had a flicker of purple sparking in the arcane blue glow which took the place of where living eyes should be. Across the field, the warmounts had raised their heads and turned toward the group.

"There's talk of either sending the children to some of their distant relatives or of marrying Agnes off to one of several anxious suitors." Bennett spit in token of their opinion on that matter. "Somewhat further down on the list is appointing someone as their guardian, to hold and work the land until Agnes or Hector come of age. I don't like the sound of that one either."

Zero and Geoffrey exchanged glances.

"And all with an eye toward getting the children out of the way and getting their land and the family money, no doubt," the younger necroknight said.

"I think someone had better remind them the MacLean bairns already have guardians," Zero growled.

"Yes," said Bennett. "Before Broken Sky does."

She pointed toward the old gray warmount who was now walking determinedly toward the village's crag-perched keep.

***

Though most of the villagers had returned to their homes in Invercraig or the surrounding farmsteads, old Thomas Fraiser, the local Deacon of the Scottish Kirk and the Shipwrights' Brotherhood, and his family had been slow to leave the great house. Suspicious of his motives, Mayor Sarah Scott and several others of the village counsel had also remained to keep the Fraisers from putting down roots.

A fortunate turn for the Fraisers as well, Zero privately thought, having spoken with the spectral Laird Craig several times. He doubted the ghostly warrior would long tolerate the presence of 'upstart Calvinist presbyters' in his home now the immediate threats to Invercraig were gone.

Still, the old deacon was currently in residence and making himself heard throughout the length of the great hall when Zero and his companions arrived. " … worthy object for your affections, Agnes MacLean."

"I'm not a prize heifer," the young woman snapped in reply, "to be auctioned off to the highest bidder,

Deacon Fraiser. An' if I was, the price certainly wouldn't go to anyone but me an' ma kin."

"Uppity tart! You would do well to remember manners in front of your betters, child. You and your brother cannot work the land yourselves. Either take an older and wiser husband to -"

"Wherever you're suggesting she take a husband, old man, it isn't going to happen without her consent," growled Aggie's brother Hector. "And you take back what you said about her being a tart while you're at it!"

"Do none of this chattel have manners?" The ancient old man glared around the great hall, but no one in his immediate vicinity would meet his eyes. "I've a mind to give you a good whipping, boy, as your unlamented father clearly should have done more often."

Zero had been quietly walking closer during the exchange. Now he growled warningly, "I think *not*!"

The small crowd, mostly Fraisers, but sprinkled with the town councilors and others, heard him and began parting, but it was Broken Sky shouldering past who really got people moving out of the way. The warmount's hooves were uncannily silent on the hall's floor as he strode forward and stood beside Hector.

While the deacon and the other men with him goggled at the warsteed, Zero, Geoffrey, and Bennett took places beside and around Aggie.

"You!" sputtered the deacon, once he noticed their arrival.

"You!" echoed Zero. "And us! Yet again!"

The necroknights had encountered the ancient Deacon Fraiser just before the undead attack on Craig House. They'd made something of an impression on each other.

"Oh, good," said Mayor Sarah. "I was hoping Sir Bennett would get you here before this farce went on much longer." Turning to the deacon, she added, "I don't want to have to remind you again, Thomas Fraiser. The girl may not yet be of age, but women and children haven't been chattel in Scotland these last hundred and some years. An' if'n they still were, you're not the one to be deciding their disposition anyway."

"They are clearly orphans of the parish," thundered Fraiser, getting going again. "And as a Deacon of the Kirk as well as the Brotherhood of Sh-"

"And you clearly have no right to be inserting yourself into this matter," Zero cut the old man off. "These children are neither part of your religion nor members of the Shipwrights' Guild. And they already have a guardian."

"You!" sputtered the deacon. "You abominations before God most clearly have no right to be here, interfering with the laws of man and nature! Get out! And take that ancient, useless beast with you!"

Broken Sky lifted his head and bared his teeth at the deacon, showing the fangs of a warmount, even if worn with long usage and age. Hector reached up and put a calming hand on his shoulder.

"Actually, Deacon Fraiser," said the young vicar Dand Woodward, "Sir Zerollen is correct. The MacLeans were never enrolled as members of the Kirk."

The deacon blinked at the vicar; his tirade knocked sideways. But he quickly recovered, turning his ire on the younger man, "Well then, boy, get to it. Shouldn't you be stepping up to save them from Godless heathenry and Papism?"

"Oh, for the Light's sake! Enough!" Zero thundered, silencing all of the hall before Broken Sky took another step toward the stubborn and pedantic old human. "Hector MacLean has been chosen by a warmount! Until he comes of age, he's under the protection of Sir Geoffrey and I."

"And the Knights of Caliburn as well," said Bennett into the silence.

Deacon Fraiser looked taken aback for a moment, but rallied smoothly. "Well, then that settles the boy's future. But we were discussing the girl and the disposition of the farmland. And as senior born, her husband would have-"

"Nothing!" Aggie snapped. "And kindly stop talkin' about me as if I'm not standing right here before ya! As if I've no rights under Queen Mary's laws. And since you keep ignoring my rights, I choose Sir Zerollen to stand as my champion to enforce them!"

The fiery-haired girl spun toward Zero, pulling a ribbon from her sleeve and tangling it among the hawthorn and rowan blooms on the hat he was carrying. "There. You're wearing my favour now."

She met his startled, arcanely-blue eyes and whispered, "You'll be my knight, won't you? Isn't this how they do it in the ballads?"

"Ah!" said Zero, less than brightly. This, he hadn't expected.

"Blasphemy!" shrieked the old deacon, who was beginning to look apoplectic as he was continually thwarted.

"Actually, no. It isn't," said Father Woodward, mildly. "Favours given knights are respectable, but not sacred."

But no one was listening to him, for Mayor Sarah spoke at almost the same time and considerably louder than the young vicar, her words clearly directed to the infuriated ancient deacon. "Hush you, Thomas Fraiser!" said Mayor Sarah. "Let's hear what our good knight has to say."

"Elf!" fumed the deacon. "Undead perversion of God's Laws -"

"Thomas! Enough!" roared Dand Woodward — to the surprise of everyone. The vicar had a fine voice and the training to project it throughout the room. "You're embarrassing the Kirk and you're embarrassing yourself. And your family. Enough, man!"

Father Woodward put a hand on the ancient old man's shoulder and another on his wrist in what Zerollen recognized as a 'come along' hold. Then the annoyed young vicar firmly walked Deacon Fraiser out of the room by the door to the tower stairs before any of his equally startled family could complain or intervene.

Where had that young man learned a peacekeeper's trick of crippling pressure on nerves and tendons?

Aggie turned back to Zero, hope and doubt warring in her expression.

"Aggie," Zero began. Paused.

"Agnes," he tried again.

Bessariel snorted explosively right next to his ear, having come as silently into the room as Broken Sky, causing her knight to jerk away in surprise.

She shouldered him further out of the way and put her head down to study Aggie, turning her horse-like head from side to side to inspect the girl with both eyes. She extended her head until her nose and fanged mouth were almost against the young woman, who was watching her with huge surprised eyes. After a timeless moment, the warmount blew a breath of warm air across the girl and turned her head back to Zero.

The black mare's expression was clear enough. Zero coughed and relaxed.

"Forgive me, Agnes. Bess has a prior claim, but she's decided you're of our pack." Zero bowed deeply in the elven fashion, drew his sword, reversed it, and dropped to one knee. He offered the human girl the hilt. "If you will accept my service, Agnes MacLean, I would be most honored and proud to act as your defender and guardian and also to extend that service to your sister Mary MacLean until such time as you release me or one of us passes beyond."

Aggie touched the hilt. "I accept," she managed to gasp out before the sword thrummed a single low note in token of witness by those Powers to whom Zero gave honor.

Once Zero had sheathed his blade, Aggie asked, "Why didn't you include Hector in your protection?"

Zero nodded to the pair of Hector and Broken Sky. The old warmount was snuffling the boy's back while Hector hugged him, leaning against his wide chest. "He already has a guardian.

"But!" Zero continued, louder for the others in the room, "Since human law isn't quite caught up to dealing with the other Folk, if and when it becomes necessary, I will act as speaker for your brother's rights." Zero loosed a dark glare at the tower stair where Deacon Fraiser and the young vicar had vanished.

"All good," said Mayor Sarah. "Let's get this into writing before that idiot Thomas slips his keepers and comes down again raving about some other point of law."

She started across the room toward the main stairs, paused, and turned back. "As for you four," she pointed to men who'd been standing nearby but trying hard not to attract attention to themselves since the warmounts had joined the proceedings. They ranged in age from a youth barely older than Aggie to a grey-haired fellow who couldn't have been much younger than the deacon himself.

The mayor continued, "You'd best prepare to present your suits to Sir Zerollen, since he'll be standing for Agnes' father and mother in this matter."

Zero gave them much the same look he'd sent after Thomas Fraiser. Only the youth had nerve enough to fully meet his stare, though the young man turned several shades paler as the necroknight studied him.

"I'll make myself available to speak with later," Zerollen told them, knowing he'd need time to clear his head before dealing with suitors for Aggie in marriage or he'd likely just kill all four of them. "Seek me out by the fireplace here tonight, if you wish."

***

"Oh! To have an image of his face when Aggie asked him to be her knight!" Bennett crowed. "And you missed it, Hrothgar!"

The knights were eating and drinking in the barrel-vaulted room near the kitchen. The room was lit with a mage light cast on the ceiling stones and was also hung with several lanterns around the walls. Despite having sat mostly abandoned since the Risen had stormed through on their search for treasures and artifacts of arcane and holy power years ago, the room was surprisingly cozy, though still in need of more cleaning than the brief influx of Invercraig's villagers had given it.

Hrothgar rolled an eye at Zero. The Dane's expression was deadpan, except for the crinkles at the corners of his eyes and a quirk at the corner of his mouth he was fighting to keep from turning into a grin. "Your hat is beginning to look very festive," he observed as dryly as he could manage.

"Two -, no, three ladies' favours," Bennett counted, grinning.

"You're just jealous, Bennett," Zero growled and curled tighter around a mug of heated ale. "And its four when you count Bess's tail hair in the hatband."

"Well, its festive now," said Geoffrey, referring to the hat. "But I can tell I'm going to have to learn more Scots. And that Highland tongue. I know I'm missing things people are saying, especially with what happened earlier."

He looked to the two Caliburn knights. "He's not explaining. Will either of you?"

"Well, our good sir knight here," said Bennett teasingly, while Zero grumbled something into his ale, "in addition to having yourself as a squire - something he'd sworn up and down he would never do - has now adopted the MacLeans as family."

"Not exactly," clarified Hrothgar. "But close enough for legal matters. And I heard you were speaking up for the boy at least, Sir Bennett. In the name of our Order."

"Would you want to argue with the choice made by a warmount, Sir Hrothgar?" Bennett asked.

"Not after the first time," said Hrothgar with a grimace. And returned to his ale.

The clatter of shoes going up and down the nearby stairs had become a background noise Zero noticed by its absence. He glanced warily toward the opening into the room.

Mayor Sarah and the town's herbalist, chief midwife and healer, Bridget Greneglais were peering back at him and his companions as though they weren't quite sure they should interrupt.

"Come! Join us, ladies," Zero called, rising to his feet and offering both of them an elven bow.

Geoffrey and Hrothgar hastily rose as well and made a leg, as did Bennett.

"Thank you, Sir Knights. I beg pardon for interrupting your breakfast and relaxation, but we have another problem which needs addressed."

"Actually, we have two," said Mayor Sarah.

"Is this about that Deacon Fraiser again," asked Zero, eyes narrowing to two bright sparks of blue.

Mayor Sarah made a face as she crossed the room. "Seriously, that Thomas Fraiser is a third problem all by himself, but one not easily solved without resort to violence."

Geoffrey coughed and politely offered the mayor his chair. Hrothgar did the same for Bridget. The knights retrieved chairs for themselves from another table.

Once everyone was seated again, Sir Bennett asked, "How may we help you, good women?"

"I'm being banished from the village," said Bridget bluntly.

"You're being *what?*" Geoffrey exclaimed.

"And I'm afraid that is extended to yourselves as well, Sir Geoffrey. Sir Zerollen," said the mayor.

Zero put a restraining hand on Geoff's arm. "I can guess what started this," he said. "After our display in the great hall this morning. And now, with the Risen having been put down and the raiders driven off, we're the most frightening possible threat left to put the villagers in fear for their lives. My raising some of the fallen, the fight between us and the resurrectionist, and the slaughter of those geese afterward …" Zero closed his eyes. It had been better than turning on the very people they'd been protecting, but it still *hurt* to lose control. Even if the geese deserved it.

Bridget said into the silence, "And I've revealed myself as a spellcaster and warrior. And the town's menfolk got to see my legs and form, albeit in armor."

She was wearing her hair neatly platted into a long rope falling over one shoulder, but still uncovered by any of the coifs or scarves or bonnets most human women habitually wore. Zero approved; it made her mildly elven features more noticeable, but no doubt emphasized her otherness to the villagers.

"But!" protested Geoffrey, more concerned about Bridget's banishment than his own. "You're their healer! And without you making lights on the clifftop, the entire castle might have been overrun with skeletons and ghouls."

"I'm afraid Bridget and Sir Zerollen have the right of it though," said Mayor Sarah. "Now the immediate enemy is gone, people are remembering what you did during the battles. And afterward. And they are afraid."

Geoff put his face in his hands.

Zero said, "I can understand why they're afraid of us. I'd rather been expecting it of them, if we didn't get ourselves out of here soon. But Healer Greneglais -"

"It's that bastard Deacon Fraiser and his ilk again," said Hrothgar unexpectedly. "And most of them are, as the lady herself pointed out, more offended she put on her armor than by any of the small magicks she cast. As if they expected her to be fighting on the hilltop in skirts and a shawl!"

"Oh, yes," said Bennett, their tone annoyed. "As if Our Good God who made us would be offended by the sight of a woman's legs or hair!"

"They haven't treated you that way," complained Geoffrey, equal parts annoyed and puzzled.

"Sir Geoff, I don't think they realize I was born a woman. I've certainly had no desire to let them see me out of my armor or otherwise enlighten them. They can ignore that question as long as I don't *flaunt it* in front of them," they finished bitterly. "But Goodwoman Bridget here - and apologies for me talking about you as though you aren't present, my dear lady - suddenly stepped out of the role everyone expected of her and became a warrior right in front of them. Now they don't know how to view her place in their little orderly world. She's gone beyond what they knew of her and, like yourselves, made them afraid. We humans don't take change well. Otherwise, two hundred and something years after the Mankiller Plague first struck, women should be ruling everywhere."

Mayor Sarah smiled

Healer Greneglais said, "That sums it up very well, Sir Bennett. Thank you. And thank you, Sir Geoffrey; your concern touches me. But a few weeks without them being able to run to me for every little thing will likely make the wiser among the town's folk see reason. And to that end, and for other reasons, I'd be willing to join the MacLean children at their farm for the spring. They should have at least one adult who can pass for human with them while you're away hunting down Dyer and what's left of his band and that Dunstan who was speaking through the necromancer you killed. Particularly if they are still spreading sickness and raising more undead wherever they go."

"I did make a promise to the Hawthorn Maid to find the resurrectionist responsible for the blighting of her tree," Zero said. "While we have one of them dead and burnt, there's whoever was possessing the body to account for yet. Dunstan, bastard son of the old Laird, or whatever he actually is or was, may also be dead or possibly disembodied, but we don't know which, if either. Or if he has other resurrectionists under his power." Zero repressed a shudder at that thought, but his expression let slip how much the idea of more of them disturbed him.

"Apparently," he continued, "Dyer and his men were somehow part of the evil Dunstan was spreading. Even without the resurrectionist around, Dyer's company is still a threat to Invercraig or any other village or steading too small to hold him off."

"I suppose all that means we still have a job to get done," said Geoffrey. "I've a few matters myself I'd like to discuss with Captain Dyer."

"Oh, we've always had a job," Zero agreed. "Now we just have a clearer direction to work in. And it's a much better use for us both than acting as couriers between Edinburgh, Invar Nis, and Thornhill. Or, somewhat sad to say, a better use for us than being farmers. We are necroknights. And when there are things which need killing, we hunt."

***

But before the hunt could begin, there were things to prepare, and Aggie's unwanted suitors to deal with. Mayor Sarah suggested both necroknights needed a new wardrobe, particularly before Zero met with Agnes' suitors again in the Great Hall. Geoffrey was particularly in need, though both had been reduced to wearing armor pieces scavenged from a dozen different sets of already mismatched gear. As for clothing, almost everything except their hats and riding capes – those items they hadn't worn in battle, that is – were in tatters.

Thus, it was later that morning, they both found themselves being measured and prodded, while the women sorted through a variety of clothing and fabric, pins, and ribbons. Unspoken between them all were the recent murders of many of Invercraig's men and uncautiously militant women by the renegade company led by Captain Dyer. The deaths had led to many families having extra clothing available to sell or reuse themselves. Plus, there was the clothing and gear stripped from the dead raiders as well.

Geoffrey confined himself to picking items salvaged from his renegade comrades until the ladies insisted he have at least one set of 'new' clothes to show his own elevated station as a knight. These would be in various Scots' tartan for the most part, helping disguise his origins on the Anglish side of the border as long as he didn't speak. Outside of Mayor Sarah Scott and her closest advisors on the town council, none of the villagers seemed aware Geoffrey had ridden with Dyer's raiders. All in on the secret had agreed the pair of necroknights had enough problems without being associated with that hated group.

Drawers, triubhas - which Geoffrey managed to pronounce as 'troovas', shirts, and jackets were all eventually found. While Zero had transferred the blackthorn and rowan blooms to his wide-brimmed Swiss citizen's hat as soon as he'd recovered it from the ladies who had cleaned and brushed the last of the whin brambles out, Geoff had found a bonnet in the MacLean tartan's green and black. One of the ladies passed him pins with which he attached some of his rowan and blackthorn blooms.

He perched it somewhat jauntily off-center on his head. It emphasized the odd green tinge his pale blond hair carried since he'd Risen. To that start of headgear, with the ladies' approval, he added an old Cavalier's hat of excellent quality. The rest of his share of the blackthorn and rowan blooms joined ostrich plumes dyed a vivid red. The pair of hats were the brightest things about his clothing choices, the rest being mostly undyed wool or linen. But while Geoffrey was scolded gently for his bland color choices, there was much talk of how they planned to brighten his clothing with the addition of some ribbons and strips of velvet and fur, and silver or cloth-covered buttons, especially to his jacket. Zero made them happier by digging about until he found items in blues and greens and some yellow leathers not yet darkened with repeated oiling.

The necroknights were sent off with orders to return after noon for more fittings. Free of the sartorial fuss, they went to find the MacLean children and help them recover their own belongings.

The two-wheeled MacLean cart had been left at the MacIvers' steading. As a result, there was bargaining to be done for the use of a new or used one to get their goods at least that far, since it was unlikely the necroknights would be tolerated in Invercraig much longer - though what, exactly, the townsfolk who wanted them out would do if they overstayed their welcome wasn't clear. The children simply couldn't abandon their beds and the other items too bulky to carry by hand which had been brought along with them. The original plan had been to wait to catch a ride partway home with the MacIvers when they came in for market day.

Off they went to the cartwright's shop, which, along with the wheelwright's, nestled in the shadow of the larger stable where most of the crown couriers' remounts were kept, along with a few horses owned by some of the wealthier citizens who still didn't have enough room to keep them at their homes. However, many of the town's carts and wagons had been damaged, if not destroyed, in the fighting, and there was a long queue of repairs to be made before even a handcart might be available.

"Maybe if Broken Sky would put up with it, we could lay the bed sacks over his back and tie them in place," Hector suggested after they'd been told how long the queue for repairs stretched out.

"It would make more sense to simply ride him out to the MacIver's and bring the cart back," Zerollen told him.

Bridget found them talking outside the cart- and wheelwright shops and reminded them she also had a wagon they would be able to use. Then she whisked Aggie and Mary-wee away for some mission of their own, leaving Hector and the necroknights to gather the children's belongings and carry them down to the Healer's home.

It was almost noon when they returned from collecting those items, Zerollen carrying the family treasure chest and some other items, Geoffrey several rolls of clothing and blankets. Broken Sky trailed along behind them with Bessariel, both mounts tolerating being blanketed with the bed sacks. Hector and Mary-wee perched on top of the sack on the old mount's back like any youngsters cadging a ride on the family plow horse. Their dog Bannock frisked alongside, happy to be doing something with his people more interesting than guarding or sorting the sheep and cattle and the remaining geese which had been packed into the Great House's stable yard.

Healer Greneglais' two assistants were packing her wagon high with her household goods which hadn't made the escape to Craig House when Invercraig had been evacuated. Many of the rest of the items already in the wagon had never been unloaded from that original retreat, save for the medicines, cloths, and splints used after the battle against the necromancer's small army of skeletons and ghouls. Zerollen and Geoffrey added their strength to the work, carrying out the heavier and bulkier of the furnishings. Included were a surprising number of casks filled with seeds of various types, all carefully labeled with names and notes in a confusing mixture of Latin, Gaelic, Anglish and other scripts.

One of her assistants explained, "She said since she wouldn't be here to plant them in the garden, to just load it all for the MacLeans' farm or wherever she'd be going."

Hector looked at the number of casks and groaned. Broken Sky lipped his shoulder gently in commiseration.

Nooning came and was long past when the knights had to be reminded to hurry back to Craig House to wash up and present themselves to their self-appointed tailors.

***

Word must have gone out through Invercraig and the re-occupied farms. By nightfall, a goodly number of the folk who had just finished decamping from the Great House were there again. This time, they were dressed in their finery to observe the proceedings.

"Looks like it still takes a whole village to arrange the betrothal of one young woman," said Geoffrey. "I'd wondered if that was just an Anglish thing."

"Makes me glad I was raised among the Folk," Zerollen replied. "You're remembering things? Were you married?"

"I *was*," Geoffrey answered with an edge in his voice. "Didn't King Henry declare any marriages to those Risen were to be considered annulled right before he died?"

"I think I heard something about that," Zero admitted.

Geoffrey didn't reply, his eyes focused on that middle-distance of memory only the one remembering can see.

In deference to the living's greater need for warmth, Zero had chosen the far end of the great hall beyond the fireplace as his post. There was a withdrawing room with a fireplace of its own there, but given it was under the damaged upper floors, no one felt bold enough to be using it. That entire end of the hall was somewhat suspect, despite the great sturdy arches of timber and stone making up the ceiling. Even Zero had only filched a chair and desk from the room rather than stay within it to write his reports.

Beyond them, the great room was bright with mage light and lanterns and the tartans and doublets and hose, and gowns of the people of Invercraig. Bennett appeared in their armor - breastplate and pauldrons freshly polished - on the main stairs for a moment, inspecting the hall. They vanished again, then reappeared in escort to Sarah Scott looking conservatively elegant in her scarlet mayor's gown.

Behind them, Aggie - no, this was definitely Agnes MacLean - appeared in a dark woad blue gown. A carefully deliberate strand of her vivid hair peeped from under her cap. A shawl of MacLean tartan wrapped her shoulders.

Bridget Greneglais followed in her dark healer's robe, but with her magelit staff prominent, and a variety of ribbons braided into her long rope-twist of coiled and pinned hair, a small beribboned hat topping it all off. They displaced the citizens gathered near the fireplace, though they ended closer to where Zero and Geoffrey stood than to the fire itself.

Zerollen touched his squire's elbow, bringing Geoff out of whatever unhappy reverie he'd been lost in.

Together, the necroknights joined the ladies. They bowed. The ladies curtsied. Bennett bowed.

All four men from the morning stepped forward from the crowd and bowed. While Zero had seen Dand, the young vicar, somewhere in the crowd, Deacon Fraiser was blissfully missing. However, Bessariel and Broken Sky had stepped in from the bailey and were currently standing guard on either side of the entry door.

Zero offered his hand to Agnes and led her forward to stand beside and slightly in front of him. He drew his sword and grounded it lightly on the stone hearth before the fireplace as Geoffrey likewise took a guard position to Agnes' right. "Gentlemen," Zero acknowledged the would-be suitors. "Present yourselves to us."

The oldest man there stepped forward. Zero guessed him at somewhere over half a century, but not too obviously. He still carried himself well and upright.

Agnes shuddered, but so carefully controlled only the necroknights noticed.

Before either side could speak, jeers went up from the bystanders. Cuckold was one of the milder insults. "You've already put two women in the ground; have done, fellow!" was one the necroknight found more alarming.

Bessariel's presence in Zero's mind shared a pointed image of a young mare kicking an older stallion in a most delicate place, causing Zero to snort a laugh even as he also winced at the image. Broken Sky did snort and give the mare a decidedly unpleased stare.

"I am Murdock Duncan Fraiser -"

"No!" said Agnes.

"No!" agreed Zero a beat after her. "None of the Deacon's ilk."

"I assure you I am -"

“I refuse!” Agnes said loudly, then continued, trying to soften her repulsion with politeness, “I’m flattered you would consider me on a par with your prior wives, but I’m too young to give you the wise counsel your years deserve, Goodman Fraiser. Surely you’ll be more comfortable in the experienced hands of your daughters-in-law’s households.”

He unexpectedly gave her a grateful look, while the crowd continued their comments. “You’re quite certain? I’ll admit I’m not so nimble as I used to be, but I can offer you a fine house and established dairy and the security of being part of the Frasier family.” He took another step closer, his voice dropping to almost a whisper, “My father put me up to this. Wouldn’t accept I’d rather honor my last wife’s memory. He’ll cause you and yours more trouble, Goodwoman MacLean. Consider yourselves warned.”

Agnes blinked in surprise. “Father Woodward?”

“Goodness, no! Thomas Fraiser is my father.”

“Your parent?”

“Yes,” Murdock Fraiser said patiently, while Zero shook his head slightly at the confusion.

“Then you canna be that old.”

“Thank you, child. I’ve reached years enough.”

“Thank you, Goodman, for the warning,” she managed to get out. “Will he make trouble for you?”

“He’ll gripe, but there’s not much he can do to me now I’ve done his bidding and embarrassed myself before the town.” He held up a hand to forestall a reply. “I remember what it was like to be young. But be careful in your choices. My father has hooks in many places.”

He gave her an age-stiffened bow. She replied with a quick bob of a curtsy. After exchanging nods with the necroknights, he made his way back into the crowd.

"Well, that was an unexpected turn of things," Agnes said quietly to Zero and Geoff. She smoothed her gown and looked inquiringly at the three men remaining.

The two fully adult men were exchanging rather heated stares with each other, while the youth eyed them askance. He seized the moment and hurriedly edged forward while they are distracted by one another.

He pulled off his bonnet and bobbed a quick bow to Zero. "Sir." And to Agnes, then in a quick rush, "I'd really like to pay court to your daughter… lady… I want to pay court to Aggie!"

He turned directly to Agnes, saying, "I'd really like to go walking with you after services Sunday, Aggie. Would you, please?"

"Benjamin Gunn," she said. "I'd love to, but I'm going back to the farm in the morning. Maybe we could after the market starts fully."

"But… That's a whole month," Benjamin said mournfully and with a touch of worry, glancing from Aggie to the two remaining suitors.

"Not that long, lad," said Zero, looking the youth over thoughtfully.

"There's more than cattle reivers come up from the Border," the young man said. He bobbed his head again and gave Zero a direct look. "Sir. I've heard tell you've been banished from Invercraig. Who'll be here to protect Aggie and her brother and sister once you're gone?"

"I don't think Invercraig's authority extends much beyond the village," Zero replied dryly. "Whether they think it does or not. But Aggie and her brother and sister *will be* protected against raiders, reivers, and anyone thinking to seize the MacLean lands by a Highland wedding."

His eyes narrowed to two slits of arcane blue fire as he studied the youth. "You clearly have something of that worrying you. So, what protection can you offer her that two necroknights cannot? And what dowry do you bring?"

"Dowry?" choked the young man.

"What skills? What wealth? What strength of arms and clan?"

The young man started to bite his lip, then straightened and met Zero's stare. "I'm Benjamin Gunn, son of Duncan Gunn of Clan Gunn. I'll have my acres next to my father's once I'm married and properly settled. Until then, I can offer my help plowing and keeping the land 'til harvest. And my good right hand in defending Aggie from those as would treat her ill."

Zero nodded. "Then you may walk out with her as she seems agreeable to it. But mind this. Walking is all you'll be doing."

"Aye, sir. I understand."

He bobbed his respects to Zero and Agnes once again and withdrew to the edge of the crowd. He seemed torn between watching Aggie or the remaining two suitors.

Both of the men had the tans which come from hours spent on the water. Both were of an indeterminate age which for humans Zero guessed at mid-twenties to early thirties. Both were dark of hair and eye. Both of a similar height and build as well though one seemed to stand a little straighter and move more as a swordsman might to Zero's eye.

There seemed little to decide between them on the surface.

And they were in such a heated argument between themselves, Zero turned to Agnes and the other women and said, "Why don't we let the two of them sort it out between themselves and see who's still standing at the end of it?"

Mayor Sarah hid a smile behind her hand. "Seems like a waste of breeding stock," she said bluntly.

"I suppose there is that," Zero agreed.

He looked over his shoulder at the two, who seemed on the verge of drawing blades on one another. "Hey! Before you go murdering each other, have you fulfilled your obligation?"

They didn't respond, so he walked closer. "Hullo! Have either of you sired children that lived?"

Agnes hid her face in her hands. Bridget and Mayor Sarah exchanged glances and chuckled. "Trust him to word it like one of the shee would."

True enough, for both men stopped and stared at the necroknight.

"Did you just ask me if I'd sired a bastard child?" demanded the man on the left.

Zero shook his head. "I asked if you'd any living children, given the age you appear."

The man who had spoken turned redder in the face than he already was.

The other chuckled and said, "Good sir knight, if I do, none of the ladies have petitioned me for support. But I'm told I have a daughter in Bristol and another in Kalay. And perhaps a son, if he's survived his infancy."

"Jackadawg!" accused the red-faced man.

"And a salty dawg at that," agreed the second in seeming affability, but his hand was near, if not actually on, his rapier. "But do tell us, Simon. Have you any bairns scattered about the coasts from your voyages?"

"Sintclair!"

"Gently, good sirs," warned Zero. "And remember, it was you who pushed this on me. Either stand down or speak up." He looked from one to the other, "You might start with introducing yourselves. I am called Sir Zerollen diGriz, Knight of the Red Horse in service to

Her Majesty Mary II, called the Fairy Queen of Scots, as courier *and* Agent of Her Will. Current Champion of Agnes MacLean. And you are?"

His emphasis on the capitals and invocation of manners seemed to remind them of their own. Both men straightened and bowed. The red-faced Simon and the one he'd named Sintclair exchanged glances. Sintclair made an 'oh, go ahead' gesture and stepped once to the side.

Red-face drew himself up to attention and said, "I am Captain Simon Munro, Master of the Winnowing and owner of half the fishing and trading fleets from Invercraig to Invar Nis. I wish to enter negotiations for the hand of your ward, Agnes MacLean. Sir!" He made a leg in the Anglish fashion.

Bessariel was watching them closely and listening through her bond with her rider. Her reaction was immediate, an image of an enraged Sheer stallion savaging a mare he was trying to mount.

Zero's reaction, but a beat after Bessariel's, was to inquire with acid sarcasm, "An' would ye be havin' any interest in the rest of her?"

Munro stared at Zero in a shocked mix of fear and horror, and other emotions which passed too rapidly to read. Sintclair made a stifled exclamation and looked like he wanted to step in again.

Zero's own sword hand had shifted toward his blade. He was aware Geoffrey had his own dangerous focus on the pair of suitors as he added, "Because milady's hands will be stayin' just where they currently are. And any negotiations for the whole package of herself will need to be directed to her as well as me."

Agnes took that as cue to proceed, beginning with asking the man pointed questions about his wealth and holdings, his principle abode, and whether any other women might sue him for support of babes he had sired. He sputtered a bit, but took the questioning with better temper than he'd shown thus far. Zero made few other comments; either Agnes' deceased mother or Bridget and Mayor Sarah had schooled her well. And since Aggie didn't have the pointed dislike Bessariel had for the man lurking in her mind, she didn't immediately dismiss his suit.

Zero determined to find out more about the man, since Bess did sometimes take an instant dislike to people Zero otherwise found decent and good. He couldn't ignore the image she'd sent him, it was far too vivid and raw an assessment of things she recognized which he couldn't. Things he couldn't yet act on without seeming irrational to both Agnes and the audience of curious townsfolk. So, after further talk, Captain Munro was added to the list of recognized suitors. He retreated only a few steps at first, listening in as Henry 'call me Harry' Sintclair made his introduction. Which was only fair in Zero's eyes, since Sintclair had been there to hear all of Munro's negotiations with Agnes. Munro continued to lurk nearby until finally, under Geoffrey's increasingly pointed regard he buggered off. Many of the small crowd had already left after Goodman Fraiser had retreated and Captain Munro's course was easily tracked through the few remaining.

Sintclair also had connections with fishing and sea trade, which was hardly surprising since his Clan had holdings along the northeastern shore all the way to Thornhill and all the way back in time to the early human kingdoms there. While Zerollen didn't know the man himself, he did know many of his kin for good and ill. They were, after all, human and as widely ranged in character as any of the elves.

When asked his interest in Agnes, he replied directly to her, "I saw you at the summer fair and my eye kept falling on you out of all the women and maids there, but I never caught a chance to speak with you before this. When I heard Old Fraiser was trying to add you to his holdings, I knew I couldn't miss my time again. I would very much like to speak with you and see if your interests coincide with mine."

Agnes replied with formal seriousness she would find this interesting and plans were made for supervised visitation.

***

That task finally done, everyone retreated to Bridget's home in Invercraig to change into traveling clothes and head to the farm. The children were carried out and tucked into nesting spots in Bridget's wagon and the small group was on their way within an hour of having reached the herbalist's house yet again for the day.

Zero ranged ahead and around the wagon as a light snow begin to fall, Bessariel a silent shadow carrying him through the chilling flakes. Bannock stayed with them, sometimes vanishing into the fall in search of hares or things larger and more threatening. Geoffrey kept watch to the rear after confirming the snow was none of Zero's doing. Broken Sky vanished into the white fall, appearing randomly to check on his boy.

They pushed on by the MacIver steading, the snow still falling but not lying on the road. Only when they were within a mile or so of the MacLean farm did the snow start to stick on the road. It was about two finger widths deep when Zero reached the farm house and made sure nothing bigger than mice had moved in while they were gone. They pulled the wagon up to the door and began moving in after that, Agnes and Bridget taking charge of the younger children and the starting of a fire in the hearth.

Geoffrey drove the team into the barn and he and Zero gave the horses a rubdown before turning them out in the paddock under Bess and Broken Sky's watch. The chickens were released into their familiar barn and settled into sleepy feathered lumps on the inner fence. Bessariel and Broken Sky had apparently decided things between themselves as to which would keep watch outside first and the old warmount followed Zerollen and Geoffrey to the house, where he carefully picked a spot in the mudroom beside the outer door, lowered his head, and immediately began to doze.

Zero and Geoffrey took over watch of the fire. Bridget and Agnes prepped a bed with warmed and cloth-wrapped stones before they carried the younger children upstairs and settled themselves for the night.

***

A week passed. Geoff and Zero repaired and rehung the door to the house. Broken Sky helped with the plowing, though Hector reported the old warmount thought it was harder than carrying a knight in battle while more boring. With his aid and Bridget's pair of geldings in rotation, the necroknights got the fields turned and manured remarkably fast. Bessariel and Hector kept a watch out for raiders or unexpected suitors. Bridget, Abby, and Mary-wee cleaned, tended the cow and her calf, hunted eggs, and found places for Bridget's goods while returning the MacLeans' possessions to their familiar spots.

The second week saw the kitchen garden weeded and expanded. Geoff taught Zero how to set and weave new tight fencing around the garden to deflect the hens and the hares Bannock or Mary-wee didn't scare off. An armed group of women came out from Invercraig to consult with their exiled midwife about herbs and babies. Several of the MacIvers visited as well, bringing cheeses to swap for eggs and early sprouted greens, but mostly to see how their returned neighbors were doing and share news.

The Lady's day later that week brought the young Invercraig reverend. Dand Woodward turned up on a rented palfrey from the stable, heralded by Bannock's barking and the cryptic warning of *Something stir*s from the warmounts.

"I should have kept the gelding Sir Bennett found for me," said Woodward, swinging down from the horse. "This one has a trot which could shake out loose teeth."

"What's brought you out to the edges of civilization, vicar?" Zero asked him

"Sirs Bennett and Hrothgar were settling more of their brethren knights at Craig House and asked if I would bring you your mail, Sir Zerollen."

Ragged eyebrow arched, Zero looked askance at the young vicar, "I have mail?"

"That you do," said Father Woodward, pulling a dispatch satchel over his head and holding it out the necroknight. "Sir Bennett just handed everything over in this bag, so I've no idea what all is in there. Though from the weight of it, I'd judge your pay or some bequest was included."

"What makes you think anyone would be sending me a bequest?" Zero asked with more than a touch of surprise and suspicion in his voice.

Woodward blinked and looked confused in return. "I did call it that, didn't I?" He sighed. "We've had so many in Invercraig since the murders done by Dyer and his men, my mind has been more full of terms of the law than of the testaments lately. I hope I'm not being prophetic."

"I hope you aren't, as well," said Zero. "Let's me get your horse to the barn. Bridget and Aggie are in the house, just give a knock. I'll be right along; I'm interested in hearing about these 'brethren' who've come to join Bennett and Hrothgar."

He slipped the satchel strap over his head — so it was held crossbody and wouldn't block his sword — before taking the reins of the livery horse and leading it off to the barn. Father Woodward looked after him as though he might follow the necroknight to the barn as well, then changed his mind and started toward the house.

Zero wasted little time in stripping the tack off the rented horse and turning it out to pasture. That done, he slipped off the satchel and began going through the packets within.

The bag of money he set aside, not quite willing to explore it yet, particularly since it bore the image of the Red Horseman in the wax seal melted over the knot holding the bag shut. "Well," he said to himself, still looking at the bag, "At least they didn't go so far as to use lead to seal it."

The more seals and ribbons involved on holding correspondence closed, the more likely it would be some sort of trouble. Zero sorted the packets into rough order by putting anything with a ribbon back in the satchel, where he didn't have to think about them for a bit longer.

Using a thumbnail for breaking a simple Scots' army seal on one of the thinnest notes as he walked, he took the less disturbing of the packets to the edge of the pasture fence, where the light was better. As he'd expected, the first letter was a confirmation of receipt of his recent courier's delivery - the one Bessariel had taken to Thornhill - and the release of his monthly pay, over Bennett's signature as his acting agent. "But that Bennett already brought me," he muttered, shifting the letter to the back of the small stack.

The second was from Warmaster Icewraith:

Hail, Zero Degrees! Brother-in-death, kindly don't be scaring us back to our graves by sending a riderless warmount ever again, you little scrawny bastard! Finish whatever trouble you've discovered and get yourself back here soon. The Red Horse returns to the Russ this summer to settle our score. Make ready. Train your pup well.

It was signed simply, *'wraith*

"Finally!" said Zero.

A moment later, he added, "Well, crap! What am I going to do about the kids?"

The third was a piece of fine rag paper with a seal at the fold over and on both edges thick enough Zero paused and brought out his boot knife to break them open. "Who in the Nine Spiraling Hells sent me this?" he asked himself before fully unfolding the page. Catching sight of the signature before he'd even deciphered the Latin, he ducked like a hawk-startled hen. "Oh! I am so fucked."

My friend, it read once he'd puzzled out the words and could imagine them spoken in the human's warm rich voice, *your Black Bess gave us quite a scare when she first turned up at Thornhill. It was fortunate Dawning Sun and I were there and could translate enough to understand you were unharmed.*

Depending on the order in which you have opened your mail, you may already know we are planning a campaign to the Russ this summer. We hope to arrive as the mud is dried and to join with our allies to recapture the relics and treasures of our people and yours and of the other kindred races so robbed of their venerated items, and to take just and proper vengeance upon the Kinslayer and his minions.

Much as I know you and the other Knights of the Red Horse wish to take a very personal part in the vengeance, being privy to other matters which also pertain to you personally, I will assure you, if you must put other duty before your desires, I will make certain none of your brothers or sisters in arms have reason to think you shirked your duty to that cause.

And also, though I believe our united cause is just and that God in his Wisdom will give aid to that cause, I also believe God gave us brain and strength of arm to make choices for ourselves and that nothing is graven in stone until afterwards. Also, that there is Wisdom in the advice to not put all of one's eggs in one basket.

If you be one of those other eggs, know you are not alone in serving in another manner and you will have support in any paths your duty takes you.

I remain always, your friend, and may God's blessing be upon you.

Tercel Davidson of the Caliburn

"Well, that's about as clear as mud," Zero muttered. "Why tell me and not Icewraith as well? Unless he's not one of those 'other eggs?'" He turned back toward the barn, staring at the satchel he'd left sitting there. He really didn't want to see what was in those remaining sealed and beribboned letters.

He was less happy once he'd read them.

One, as Sir Tercel had warned, was a formal announcement to all the free necroknights to gather at their various chapter houses and prepare for war. One was from the Warmasters of the Red Horse, ordering him to present himself and his 'pup', meaning Geoffrey, to be judged on the necessity of having created another necroknight and to see if this new knight was fit to be counted among their number. The last – even more terrifying than seeing Tercel's signature – had been from the Queen, herself, requesting he return to Edinburgh as soon as possible and to join her at court 'by whatever means necessary upon your arrival.'

"Oh, that can't mean anything good."

"What can't?" asked Geoffrey as he walked in the other end of the barn, followed by Hector on Broken Sky and Bessariel trailing behind. "These two," Geoff pointed over his shoulder, "just did another of those 'something stirs' comments, loud enough I could hear them. And the last time—"

"The last time they did that, we had necromancers and ghouls come through," said Hector. "What's wrong, Zero?"

"They say a dog with more than one master never knows which way to wag his tail," said Zero as he tucked the orders back into the dispatch satchel. "Now I know how the dog feels."

"Ah!" said Geoffrey. "Care to explain that?

"Once I've done a scan to make sure we're not in for another attack," Zero promised, hurrying to Bess as she dropped down into a bow to let him mount. "I'd thought it was just about the vicar arriving, but if Bess and Broken Sky told you and Hector as well it could be something more. Go warn your sisters, Hector!"

Wrapping his fingers in the black warmount's mane and squeezing tightly with his legs, Zero kept his seat as the mare scrambled up and bolted out the back of the barn, clearing the pasture fence with plenty of room. She startled the cow and calf and spooked the newly released livery horse into bolting across the field to join Bridget's pair of geldings. Bess took the fence at the far end of the paddock and began dodging through the small trees and scrub until she came out at the top of the woodlot on the upper edge of the MacLeans' fields.

The mare picked her way carefully across the open ground, despite Zero's complaints anything could see them out there. She finally stopped at the overgrown hedge and partial stone row separating the MacLean land from what had likely once belong to Laird Craig or to the Crown.

"What is this all about?" Zero grumbled.

Bessariel whirled and turned to face the sea, almost unseating Zero in her excitement.

Broken Sky stepped out of the Hidden Ways beside them, Hector, wide-eyed, still mounted on his back, and Geoffrey, staggering a bit, having been pulled along when Broken Sky opened the Path.

Look! radiated from the pair of warmounts.

Far out on the horizon silver sails – silver, not white – gleamed in a patch of sunlight. Seven ships, visible mainly by the light on their sails, sailed north. The warmounts and their partners watched in silence until the last silvery sail vanished.

"That was beautiful. But what was it?" asked Geoffrey.

"The warships of Tir na Bretagne and the Southern Isles, likely sailing to Tir na Scota," said Zero.

"Why would they do that?" asked Hector. "Are they at war? Like Angland is with Espanya?"

"No, I think not. This spring the Kindred Races gather for war, but not with each other. This spring we prepare to return to the Russ."

"How do you know?"

"Because among the Shee, red sails are for war. And because Dand Woodward brought me my mail."

Rillan macDhai was born on the west coast of Florida. They've been telling stories since they could talk. They've been writing them down since they were given their first typewriter.

Specializing in world folklore and mythology, macDhai earned a B.A. in English from Pennsylvania State University and a minor in World Literature. Previously, they've published in Ellery Queen's Mystery Magazine as Yancey Davidson and in Tomorrow – Speculative Fiction under their own name.

Wall of Thorns and Other Stories is macDhai's first published book and currently available in paperback or on Kindle. **Wall** is a collection of the author's previously published short stories as well as several never-before- published stories which are part of the history and mythology of the world you've just visited in **Sympathy For the Living**.

On a small farm in central Pennsylvania, macDhai lives with their spouse and an everchanging number of dogs, cats, horses, and housemates. Currently they are creating the second book of the tales of Zerollen diGriz and his companions.

Made in the USA
Middletown, DE
25 October 2022